INSIGHTS INTO
HEALTHCARE
LEADERSHIP

Mohammed Basha, MSc, PhD

Table of Contents

Introduction

Healthcare, like every other industry, is evolving. The unprecedented changes in the way healthcare advances push every leader in the field to match the same pace to handle these changes. However, these changes, whatever they are, cannot weaken the importance of mastering the essentials. Your existing skills and knowledge are invaluable in this evolving landscape.

Healthcare demands are changing and escalating due to many factors. To mention a few, changes in the structure of demographics worldwide, an increase in the burden of chronic diseases, and the booming advanced technology. These are just a few items from a longer list that render healthcare complex.

Being a successful leader in healthcare is not easy. It takes sound effort and time to master the necessary skills and adopt the competencies required to work effectively in the field.

This book is not just a collection of theoretical principles. It is a practical guide designed to engage you in a way that allows you to immediately apply the concepts presented in your leadership roles within the healthcare sector. The content is supported by evidence derived from literature, ensuring its relevance and applicability.

The book is not aimed at teaching management skills or being another source of theoretical leadership principles. Tens of excellent resources provide this kind of material. However, the book intends to provide current or potential healthcare leaders with a practical review of essential concepts and tips that could significantly improve their leadership skills and positively impact their teams and organizations.

Mohammed Basha, MSc, PhD

January 2025

Acknowledgment

I want to thank Dr Omnia Hussien, who has been a core pillar for developing this book. Dr Omnia has been a great help at all stages of producing this book, from the literature review to the enhancement of the arrangement and the content.

Also, I want to thank Eng. Jihad Mohamed, whose contribution always adds great value to my work. Her help with the design and production is a fantastic mixture of professionalism and delicate art.

Section One:

Fundamentals of Leadership in Healthcare

Chapter 1: Introduction to Leadership in Healthcare

1.1   Definition and Importance of Leadership in Healthcare

Effective leadership is vital for succeeding organizations in healthcare or any other field. No single organization can make its way up to success without having clear, mindful leadership paving the way to achieve its targets. This is much needed now amid the unprecedented pace of change.

When it comes to healthcare, there are still many commonalities with other industries; however, differences also should be considered. Healthcare is a unique industry with many factors interplaying together. The global trend to privatize healthcare organizations in different countries adds complexity to this unique nature of the field. Consequently, healthcare leaders should be aware of all these interacting factors to ensure that they satisfactorily achieve the objectives of different stakeholders, which sometimes have an implicit or explicit conflict of interest.

A straightforward example is working hard to keep a healthcare business profitable while maintaining high-quality and safe patient service. Taking it superficially, it looks hard to achieve because providing a high-quality, safe service entails higher expenses, leading to decreased profits. However, this is not always the case. As mentioned, the healthcare field is unique and has its nature and, hence, its principles to achieve success. However, dealing with or trying to lead healthcare organizations as a factory might serve to achieve quick gains but eventually will ruin the whole business.

This book will explore the core insights for successfully leading a healthcare organization. These insights do not represent an exhaustive list of all you need to be an effective healthcare leader; however, they aim to represent top-priority concepts to understand and apply to be a successful leader in the field.

The concept of leadership has been extensively explored in literature, with diverse perspectives on its definition. Some interpretations have gained prominence due to the influence of their authors. Warren Bennis, a renowned pioneer in leadership studies, described leadership as the ability to understand oneself, communicate a sharp vision, build trust among peers, and take decisive actions to fulfill one's leadership potential.

From another perspective, Peter Drucker, often regarded as the father of modern management, succinctly defined a leader as "someone who has followers" and distinguished leadership from management by stating, "Management is doing things right; leadership is doing the right things." More recently, Kouzes and Posner emphasized the behavioral aspects of leadership, asserting that "leadership can happen at any time, anywhere, and in any role (Kumar & Khiljee, 2015, p. 63).

Why leadership is critical for improving patient outcomes and team performance, a few reasons are:

• **Driving Quality Improvement:** Leadership is essential to initiating and sustaining quality improvement programs within healthcare settings. Effective leaders address systemic issues and inspire teams to adopt changes that enhance care delivery and patient outcomes. Leaders are always eager to make the environment around them better than stable.

• **Overcoming Resistance to Change:** Leadership helps tackle common barriers, such as staff resistance to change, by promoting an inclusive approach and engaging healthcare professionals in transformation.

• **Engaging Teams:** Strong leadership fosters a sense of ownership among team members, encouraging collaboration and alignment with organizational goals, which improves overall team performance.

• **Promoting Efficiency and Productivity:** Leadership is vital in navigating the increasing demands on healthcare systems by implementing strategies to enhance efficiency while maintaining high standards of patient care.

• **Transformational Leadership as Change Agents:** Leaders who inspire and motivate their teams create a shared vision, address challenges collaboratively, and foster a culture of continuous improvement that positively impacts team dynamics and patient outcomes.

1.2 Dimensions of Healthcare Leadership (Healthcare Leadership Model)

Different good models aim to summarise what is essential in leadership development. The Healthcare Leadership Model is a good example of the same model. The NHS Leadership Academy developed it to help healthcare leaders develop their leadership capacity guided by a well-designed framework. The model introduces nine pillars for healthcare leadership development:

1. **Leading with Care:** Supporting team members and fostering a caring environment.

2. **Sharing the Vision:** Clear, inspiring communication for long-term goals.

3. **Engaging the Team:** Building trust and encouraging participation.

4. **Influencing for Results:** Adapting to others and fostering collaboration.

5. **Evaluating Information:** Sourcing and utilizing diverse information creatively.

6. **Inspiring Shared Purpose:** Aligning with values and taking courageous actions.

7. **Connecting Our Service:** Understanding system interrelations and adopting best practices.

8. **Developing Capability:** Encouraging skill development for long-term success.

9. **Holding to Account:** Setting clear expectations and driving continuous improvement.

1.3 Leadership vs. Management

According to a report by Northeastern University (2024), healthcare leadership and management serve distinct but complementary roles in healthcare organizations. While both fall under the umbrella of healthcare administration, their focus and responsibilities differ significantly:

Key Responsibilities of Healthcare Leaders

1. Identifying Opportunities:
Leaders assess external factors like evolving healthcare regulations, patient care innovations, and technological advancements to spot opportunities for growth and improvement.

2. Visionary Thinking:
They provide a long-term vision for the organization. This vision becomes the guiding star for all strategic decisions and actions, ensuring that the healthcare facility remains relevant and competitive in a rapidly changing industry.

3. Inspiring and Motivating:
Leaders have a unique role in motivating teams by instilling a sense of purpose and direction. Their passion and commitment to the organization's vision inspire others to take ownership of the goals and work together to achieve them.

4. Fostering Innovation:
A key trait of effective leaders is their ability to encourage innovation. They support exploring innovative ideas, methodologies, and technologies to improve patient care, reduce costs, or enhance operational efficiencies.

Key Responsibilities of Healthcare Managers

1. Execution of Plans:
Managers take the strategic vision created by leaders and translate it into actionable tasks. They ensure that all aspects of the healthcare facility, from patient care to administrative operations, run smoothly and are aligned with the organization's goals.

2. Resource Management:
Managers are responsible for allocating resources efficiently. This includes managing budgets, staffing levels, equipment, and facilities to meet the organization's operational needs.

3. Staff Supervision:
Managers directly oversee staff performance, providing the necessary support, training, and development to ensure employees meet the healthcare facility's standards. They also handle administrative duties, such as scheduling and addressing performance issues.

4. Problem Solving:
Managers deal with immediate challenges and operational issues as they arise. Whether it's a patient care problem, staffing shortage, or regulatory compliance issue, managers must quickly and effectively address these concerns.

Hence, the two roles are different, albeit connected. Leaders focus on working towards ever-stretching goals involving guiding and empowering their teams. On the other hand, managers usually focus on efficiently utilizing the resources available to achieve organizational goals.

1.4 Understanding Complementary Roles.

The Interdependence of Leadership and Management

While leaders and managers have distinct responsibilities, their roles are inherently complementary. A healthcare organization requires both to function effectively and achieve long-term success.

• Leaders drive change and innovation: Leaders define the organization's direction, set new goals, and adjust strategies based on trends and opportunities. They push the boundaries and motivate the entire organization to embrace these changes.

• Managers ensure stability and consistency: Managers are the ones who keep things running smoothly in the day-to-day operations. They are responsible for implementing the changes leaders envision and ensuring that the organization operates efficiently while maintaining high-quality care.

1.5 Why Leadership Without Management Can Be Ineffective

When healthcare leaders are focused solely on developing visionary strategies without considering the practicalities of execution, it can result in unrealistic plans that cannot be implemented effectively. For example, a leader may push to adopt an innovative technology. Still, without managerial input, the required infrastructure, training, and resources may not be in place to support its success. This disconnection between strategy and execution leads to frustration and inefficiency, undermining the organization's goals.

Strategies can remain theoretical without management and may never materialize into tangible outcomes. For example, a hospital may want to improve patient satisfaction, but without adequate staff, processes, and patient flow management, the desired improvements will not happen.

1.6 Why Management Without Leadership Can Lead to Stagnation

Conversely, managers without leadership can focus too heavily on maintaining the status quo. While operational efficiency is essential, solely focusing on the present can result in missed opportunities for improvement, growth, and adaptation. Healthcare organizations that only rely on management risk becoming complacent and resistant to change, ultimately leading to stagnation.

For example, a manager may ensure the facility complies with existing regulations. Still, without leadership to push for innovation or respond to external changes, the organization may fail to stay competitive or meet evolving patient needs. Without leadership's vision, managers may lack the direction to challenge existing practices, explore new ways to improve care or adapt to new healthcare models.

1.7 The Balance Between Leadership and Management

In summary, leaders and managers have distinct yet complementary roles within healthcare organizations. Leaders set the direction, inspire innovation, and navigate external challenges, while managers execute plans, coordinate resources, and ensure efficient daily operations. Effective healthcare organizations need both. They need leadership to provide vision and inspire change, and management must implement those changes efficiently and effectively. When these roles are balanced and work in tandem, healthcare organizations are better positioned to meet the needs of patients, achieve operational excellence, and thrive in an ever-changing environment.

1.8 When to lead and when to manage effectively

While leaders' mental setup focuses on vision, strategy, and inspiration, managers' focus is on execution, structure, and day-to-day operations. Healthcare leaders and managers must work together to ensure an organization stays efficient while progressing toward its long-term goals.

• Leading when innovation and strategic direction are needed: Leadership must steer the organization through change when implementing new patient care models or responding to health crises (such as a pandemic).

• Managing when stability and operational effectiveness are essential: When staffing levels need adjustment or regulatory compliance must be met, management ensures that processes are followed.

Again, this does not imply that a healthcare manager should switch on-off modes between management and leadership. However, they should know that management and leadership skills entail complementary roles, sometimes needed to get the best results under different business conditions.

In many cases, the best healthcare leaders understand the importance of leading and managing. A leader who understands management can effectively implement their vision, while a manager with leadership skills can anticipate and prepare for future challenges. Balancing both functions allows healthcare organizations to not only meet the demands of today but also prepare for the needs of tomorrow.

Chapter 2: Key healthcare leadership competencies

Effective leaders have shared skills in common. These skills are among the necessary tools to handle their daily commitments to their organizations and teams. The following are among the top skills needed:

2.1 Visualization

If a single characteristic differentiates leaders from regular managers, it would be their ability to visualize the future. They can visualize their success, their teams' success, and their organizations' success. Leaders are adept at imagining the future. This skill is inevitable to any successful leader. We are mainly driven by our mindsets, primarily impacted by our visualization of the future. Visualization success can do miracles when planning to convert such a vision into reality.

2.2 Communication

Effective communication is a foundational skill for healthcare leaders, enabling them to convey clear goals, coordinate multidisciplinary teams, and build trust with patients and stakeholders. Miscommunication in healthcare settings is a leading cause of errors and inefficiencies (The Joint Commission, 2015). Leaders must foster open communication channels to align organizational strategies and ensure patient-centered care. Furthermore, communication is not limited to verbal exchanges; it includes active listening, cultural sensitivity, and nonverbal cues, all of which enhance collaboration in diverse healthcare environments (Glickman et al., 2007). Modern healthcare demands communication that adapts to technological platforms, such as telehealth, making digital literacy an essential subset of this competency.

2.3 Change Management

Healthcare leaders must navigate organizational and systemic changes, particularly in response to shifting policies, emerging technologies, and population health challenges. Kotter's Eight-Step Process for Leading Change (1996) remains a seminal framework, emphasizing the importance of creating urgency, building coalitions, and empowering action. These principles are particularly relevant in healthcare during large-scale transitions, such as implementing electronic health records (EHRs) or adapting to value-based care models. Leaders who excel in change management ensure smooth transitions by anticipating resistance and fostering a culture of adaptability (McAlearney et al., 2013). This competency is critical in addressing burnout and maintaining staff morale during periods of uncertainty.

2.4 Emotional Intelligence (EI)

Emotional intelligence (EI), first popularised by Daniel Goleman (1995), has become a vital competency in healthcare leadership. EI encompasses self-awareness, self-regulation, empathy, social skills, and motivation, enabling leaders to navigate interpersonal relationships effectively. Healthcare environments often involve high stress, making EI critical for de-escalating conflicts, fostering team cohesion, and promoting a supportive culture (Codier et al., 2009). Leaders with high EI are better equipped to understand the emotional needs of their teams and patients, which is linked to improved satisfaction and reduced staff turnover. Moreover, EI supports resilience, helping leaders maintain composure and decision-making capacity in crises.

1. Emotional Intelligence (EI) is Important for Leadership
Hospitalist medical directors emphasized the significance of EI for leadership, rating nearly all EI skills as essential. The only exceptions were "using a wide variety of feeling words" and "talking about anxiety," which scored lower due to potential biases stemming from physician training and education (Cherry, 2021; McMullen, 2002).

2. Self-Perception of EI

In a study by Cherry (2021), participants ranked their EI performance lower than the importance they assigned to EI in leadership, indicating awareness of the need for improvement. This suggests the potential benefits of EI development programs tailored for physician leaders.

3. Proposed EI Training and Development Methods

o Incorporating EI training in medical school curricula.

o Offering workshops and seminars as continuing education.

o Providing one-on-one leadership coaching focusing on EI concepts and self-awareness activities (Cherry, 2021).

4. Potential Impact of EI on Physician Leadership

EI has been shown to enhance physician-patient interactions and could similarly improve interactions with colleagues and stakeholders, positively impacting healthcare organizations (Cherry, 2021; Austin et al., 2007; Deshpande & Joseph, 2009).

2.5 Working with Data

Data-driven decision-making is a cornerstone of modern healthcare leadership, reflecting the shift toward evidence-based management. Leaders must interpret complex data and translate it into actionable insights that improve patient outcomes and operational efficiency (Raghupathi & Raghupathi, 2014). This competency is especially critical in the era of big data and artificial intelligence, where leaders are tasked with navigating vast datasets, ensuring data integrity, and applying predictive analytics. Additionally, working with data fosters transparency and accountability, allowing organizations to measure performance against key metrics and respond proactively to trends.

2.5 Case Study: Emotional Intelligence in Healthcare Leadership

During a sudden surge inpatient admission, a hospital unit faced overwhelming workloads and rising staff burnout. The unit leader, Dr. Emily, displayed high Emotional Intelligence (EI) by empathizing with her team's concerns. She held an open discussion to acknowledge their struggles, proposed actionable solutions to redistribute tasks, and encouraged collaboration. Maintaining a calm and supportive demeanor boosted morale and strengthened team dynamics. Her proactive communication and conflict resolution helped the team maintain high patient care standards despite the challenging situation.

Dr. Mark, known for his low EI, responded differently in a similar unit. He dismissed staff concerns as unimportant and avoided direct communication about the issues. His vague instructions and lack of acknowledgment of team emotions caused frustration and resentment among the staff. As conflicts arose, Dr. Mark's unwillingness to mediate escalated tensions, reducing teamwork and declining patient care quality. Several staff members ultimately resigned, further worsening the situation.

Discussion Questions

1. How did Dr. Emily's high EI contribute to better team performance and patient outcomes?

2. What specific behaviors of Dr. Mark reflect low EI, and how did these behaviors impact his unit?

3. How could leadership training in EI help prevent outcomes like those in Dr. Mark's unit?

4. How can organizations ensure leaders have strong EI skills?

The role of Emotional Intelligence (EI) in fostering the excellence of healthcare leaders

1. Enhances Interpersonal Relationships

• Effective Communication: EI helps leaders communicate effectively with diverse stakeholders, including patients, staff, and executives. Emotionally intelligent leaders can convey empathy, understanding, and clarity, building trust and rapport.

• Conflict Resolution: EI enables leaders to manage and resolve conflicts constructively by recognizing and addressing the emotional undercurrents driving disagreements.

2. Improves Decision-Making

• Self-awareness: EI fosters self-awareness, allowing leaders to recognize their emotional triggers and biases. This leads to more objective and thoughtful decision-making.

• Empathy in Decision-Making: Emotionally intelligent leaders consider the impact of their decisions on others, promoting fairness and inclusivity.

3. Promotes Organizational Performance

• Team Building: EI strengthens team dynamics by fostering an environment of collaboration and mutual respect. Leaders with high EI can inspire and motivate teams, enhancing productivity and morale.

• Change Management: Healthcare is a rapidly evolving field, and EI helps leaders manage organizational change by addressing resistance and guiding teams through transitions with empathy and resilience.

4. Facilitates Patient-Centred Care

• EI has been linked to improved physician-patient interactions, as leaders with high EI can model empathetic behavior that cascades throughout their teams. This fosters a culture of patient-centered care, enhancing patient satisfaction and outcomes.

5. Supports Stress and Crisis Management

• Emotional Regulation: In high-stress healthcare environments, emotionally intelligent leaders remain calm and composed, helping their teams stay focused and effective.

• Resilience Building: EI aids in developing resilience, allowing leaders to bounce back from challenges and setbacks.

6. Drives Leadership Development

• Self-Improvement: EI encourages leaders to engage in continuous self-reflection and personal development, enhancing their leadership capabilities over time.

• Training and Coaching: EI skills can be cultivated through targeted training, workshops, and coaching, further strengthening a leader's effectiveness.

2.6 Quick Check

1. Which of the following best describes the key distinction between leadership and management in healthcare?

A. Leadership focuses on operational tasks, while management focuses on long-term vision.
B. Leadership is about doing things right, while management is doing the right things.
C. Leadership inspires change and innovation, while management ensures stability and efficiency.
D. Leadership handles day-to-day operations, while management focuses on emotional intelligence.

2. Why is leadership critical for improving patient outcomes and team performance?

A. It emphasizes maintaining strict compliance with regulations.
B. It focuses solely on individual performance reviews.
C. It fosters collaboration, drives quality improvements, and overcomes resistance to change.
D. It prioritizes administrative efficiency over patient care.

3. Which of the following is NOT one of the dimensions of the Healthcare Leadership Model?

A. Sharing the Vision
B. Leading with Care
C. Building Financial Systems
D. Inspiring Shared Purpose

4. What is a key advantage of emotional intelligence (EI) in healthcare leadership?

A. Ensures adherence to clinical protocols.
B. Improves interpersonal relationships, team performance, and decision-making.
C. Replaces the need for technical and managerial skills.
D. Limits the emotional involvement of healthcare leaders.

5. What is an example of when healthcare leaders should focus on management rather than leadership?

A. Creating a strategic vision for the organization.
B. Responding to a public health crisis.
C. Addressing staffing shortages to maintain operational effectiveness.
D. Inspiring innovation in patient care delivery.

Correct Answers:

1- C

2- C

3- C

4- B

5- C

Chapter 3: Understanding Leadership: Core Leadership Theories

3.1 Leadership theories

Before discussing different theories of leadership, let us first explain the nature of a theory. Theories are generally a set of propositions that might be true or false. They are usually developed to understand a phenomenon we experience. In social sciences like leadership and management, theories are developed for similar reasons.

The following theories have been developed over different periods to explain what leadership is and how it works. The evolution of a new theory does not entail that its predecessor is wrong or faulty. However, it is a natural development of the leadership concepts that stem from our evolving understanding of the different factors involved in leadership.

The literature on leadership identifies several foundational theories widely recognized as default frameworks for understanding leadership. These include the Great Man Theory, Trait Theories, Behavioural Theories, situational and Contingency Theories, and Transformational and Transactional Leadership Theories. Together, these theories provide a comprehensive perspective on the evolution and complexity of leadership (Benmira & Agboola, 2021).

Grand Man Theory (1840s)

Key Idea: Leaders are born, not made.

• Explanation: This theory posits that leadership is an innate quality bestowed upon select individuals, often viewed as natural-born leaders with unique, divine-like traits. Historical examples include figures like Julius Caesar, Abraham Lincoln, and Mahatma Gandhi, who were considered destined to lead due to their exceptional characteristics.

• Limitations: It overlooks environmental factors, training, and development, assuming leadership cannot be learned.

Trait Theories (1930s–1940s)

Key Idea: Leadership traits can be inherent or developed.

• Explanation: This approach identifies certain personality traits, such as confidence, intelligence, and social skills, common among effective leaders. It suggests that people can inherit or acquire these traits through learning and experience.

• Applications: Modern psychometric tools for recruitment and development draw on trait theory principles.

• Limitations: Fails to produce consistent universal traits applicable across all leaders and situations.

Behavioural Theories (1940s–1950s)

Key Idea: Leadership is learned by focusing on actions rather than traits.

• Explanation: Leadership effectiveness depends on behaviors, such as decision-making, communication, and motivation. Patterns of behavior are grouped into styles, like task-oriented or relationship-oriented leadership.

• Example: Blake and Mouton's Managerial Grid evaluates leadership styles based on concern for people vs. concern for production.

• Limitations: Largely ignores the role of situational factors in leadership.

Situational and Contingency Theories (1960s)

Key Idea: Leadership effectiveness depends on the situation.

• Explanation: Leaders must adapt their style to the context, such as the team's needs, organizational culture, or external environment. The best approach depends on factors like task complexity and follower readiness.

• Example: Fred Fiedler's Contingency Model, which asserts that leaders are most effective when their style matches the situation.

Leaders are encouraged to seek environments where they can succeed rather than trying to change their style.

• Limitations: Overlooks the potential for leaders to grow and adapt beyond their inherent style.

Transformational Leadership (1990s)

Key Idea: Leaders inspire and motivate to drive change and innovation.

• Explanation: Transformational leaders focus on vision, fostering creativity, and empowering followers to exceed expectations. This approach is ideal for organizations undergoing meaningful change or seeking innovation.

• Examples: Visionaries like Steve Jobs and Bill Gates who encouraged followers to embrace change and innovation.

• Applications: Common in dynamic industries like technology and startups.

• Limitations: This may not work well in stable environments where maintaining the status quo is more critical.

Transactional Leadership (1990s)

Key Idea: Leadership focuses on structure, rewards, and performance.

• Explanation: Transactional leaders use authority to maintain order, rewarding employees for meeting objectives and disciplining those who fail. This style emphasizes clear roles, supervision, and a focus on goals.

• Examples: Managers focusing on process adherence and performance metrics in mature organizations.

• Applications: Best suited for stable organizations with clear objectives.

• Limitations: Less effective in fostering innovation or addressing rapidly changing environments.

New Leadership Approaches (2000s and beyond)

Key Idea: Leadership is a multidimensional and systemic interaction.

• Explanation: Modern theories integrate elements of transformational, transactional, and situational leadership, reflecting the complexity of today's globalized and rapidly changing world. Agile methodologies and Lean strategies support flexibility, collaboration, and responsiveness to innovation.

• Applications: Used in industries facing disruptive changes, such as technology and healthcare.

• Limitations: Adopting these new leadership approaches necessitates high adaptability and coordination, which may pose a challenge for some leaders and organizations. However, this challenge can also be viewed as an opportunity for growth and development.

Servant Leadership in Healthcare

Servant leadership in healthcare is a leadership philosophy where the leader prioritizes serving others, emphasizing the growth and well-being of their team members. This approach enhances organizational culture by focusing on empathy, ethical behavior, and fostering collaboration. Leaders are viewed as stewards who facilitate decision-making and promote trust. Research has shown that servant leadership leads to higher employee engagement, better patient care, and improved job satisfaction (Patterson, 2003; Van Dierendonck, 2011). By fostering a caring environment, servant leadership can address key challenges in healthcare settings, including burnout and staff turnover.

Situational Leadership

Situational leadership in healthcare involves adapting leadership styles based on the team's capabilities and the specific challenges of the healthcare context. Leaders assess the readiness of their team members and adjust their approach, ranging from directing to delegating. This style encourages flexibility while ensuring clarity in decision-making, allowing leaders to effectively manage diverse situations and maintain a focus on patient outcomes (Hersey & Blanchard, 1969; Goleman, 2000). By balancing adaptability and decisive actions, situational leadership enhances team performance and organizational effectiveness.

3.2 Quick Check

1. Which leadership theory focuses on leaders' ability to inspire and motivate followers by setting a vision and providing individualized support?

a) Transactional Leadership

b) Transformational Leadership

c) Situational Leadership

d) Contingency Theory

2. According to Trait Theory, which of the following is considered an essential leadership trait?

a) Ability to delegate tasks

b) Empathy and self-awareness

c) Physical fitness

d) financial knowledge

3. In which leadership theory do leaders adjust their style based on the situation and the maturity level of their followers?

a) Transformational Leadership

b) Situational Leadership

c) Path-Goal Theory

d) Leader-Member Exchange Theory

4. Which leadership style emphasizes clear structure, rules, and performance targets, typically used in situations requiring immediate results?

a) Transactional Leadership

b) Servant Leadership

c) Democratic Leadership

d) Transformational Leadership

5. According to the Leader-Member Exchange (LMX) Theory, the leader's relationship with followers is most effective when:

a) All followers are treated the same

b) Leaders and followers form close, individualized relationships

c) Followers are given full autonomy

d) Leaders focus on the task and ignore follower relationships

Correct answers:

1 - b

2 - b

3 - b

4 - a

5 - b

3.3 Case Study: Transformational Leadership in a Public Hospital

Background: A public hospital in a major city has been facing numerous challenges, including high staff turnover, low employee morale, and inefficient communication. The hospital management implemented a leadership development program to improve team performance and patient care outcomes.

The hospital's new director, Dr. Laura Evans, has a background in Transformational Leadership. She is passionate about inspiring staff to reach their full potential and fostering a sense of shared purpose. Dr. Evans has already begun to implement several changes, including:

• Developing a sharp vision: Dr. Evans introduced a new hospital-wide mission focused on patient-centered care and staff empowerment.

• Promoting innovation: She encourages staff to suggest ideas for improving patient care and workflow processes, fostering a culture of creativity and problem-solving.

• Providing individualized support: Dr. Evans conducts regular one-on-one meetings with key staff members to discuss their career development and challenges.

Despite these efforts, the hospital has faced resistance, especially from long-time employees accustomed to a more traditional, hierarchical management style. Some argue that Dr. Evans' approach lacks clarity and does not address the hospital's immediate, day-to-day operational needs.

Discussion Questions:

1. How does Transformational Leadership contribute to Dr. Evans' approach in this case, and what are the potential benefits for the hospital's staff and patient care? The potential benefits of Transformational Leadership, such as increased staff motivation and improved patient care, can bring a sense of optimism and hope for the hospital's future.

2. What challenges might arise from Dr. Evans' leadership style, especially considering the resistance from long-time employees? By acknowledging these potential challenges, the audience can better understand the complexities of leadership in healthcare and be prepared to address them.

3. How might the Situational Leadership Theory apply in this case? Could Dr. Evans benefit from adapting her leadership style depending on the situation?

4. What role do Trait Theories play in Dr. Evans' leadership effectiveness? Are there any specific traits that have helped her to initiate these changes successfully?

5. What are the limitations of Transformational Leadership in a healthcare setting, and how might Dr. Evans balance this approach with other leadership theories to address immediate operational needs?

Chapter 4: Leadership Styles, Followers, and Context

4.1 Overview of Leadership Styles

There is a myriad of identified leadership styles. A leadership style refers to a combination of specific attitudes and behaviors that an individual leader assumes. One misconception about leadership styles is that they are a permanent stigma of particular leaders, which is invalid. An effective leader can take more than one leadership style according to the different nature of the followers and the context.

While the leadership literature commonly highlights three key leadership styles, autocratic, democratic, and laissez-faire, Olatoye, Elufioye, Okoye, Nwankwo, & Oladapo (2024) suggested a broader range of leadership approaches in healthcare. These include:

Transformational Leadership style: In healthcare, this style focuses on inspiring and motivating staff to share a vision and foster long-term goals and innovation. By promoting commitment, this leadership style enhances organizational performance and patient outcomes.

Transactional Leadership style: is based on clear exchanges: rewards for performance and consequences for noncompliance. While efficient for task completion, it may hinder adaptability.

Servant Leadership style: prioritizes empathy and collaboration, creating a supportive environment where leaders focus on meeting the needs of their team, improving morale and patient care.

Distributed Leadership style: empowers teams by delegating decision-making and fostering a collaborative environment where professionals contribute equally.

Autocratic Leadership style: centralizes decision-making for efficiency in urgent situations but can diminish motivation when overused.

Democratic Leadership style: This style encourages team collaboration and inclusivity in decision-making, boosting morale, but may be slow in emergencies.

Laissez-faire Leadership style: gives autonomy to team members but can lack direction without adequate guidance.

Adaptive Leadership style: thrives on addressing evolving challenges by promoting a learning culture and empowering professionals to solve problems.

Situational Leadership style: requires leaders to adjust their style based on team readiness and specific tasks, offering flexibility in dynamic healthcare environments.

4.2 Strengths and limitations of each style in healthcare settings

Transformational Leadership: Transformational leadership significantly enhances healthcare management by motivating staff, fostering innovation, and promoting a shared vision. This approach can lead to increased job satisfaction and improved patient outcomes. However, if not carefully balanced, it may neglect day-to-day operations, and its elevated expectations can cause stress among staff (Nauman et al., 2022).

Transactional Leadership: This style focuses on clear expectations, rewards, and penalties, ensuring task completion and efficiency. While effective in stable environments, it can limit creativity and motivation and is often seen as bureaucratic (Olatoye et al., 2024).

Servant Leadership: Servant leadership prioritizes empathy and collaboration, improving staff satisfaction and patient care. However, overemphasizing service can lead to delayed decision-making and reduced organizational discipline (Nauman et al., 2022).

Distributed Leadership: This style promotes shared responsibility and decision-making, enhancing adaptability and innovation. However, clear communication is required to avoid confusion and misdirection (Quek et al., 2021).

Autocratic Leadership: Autocratic leadership is effective in urgent situations, ensuring fast decision-making. However, it may reduce morale and hinder creativity when overused, leading to disengagement (Olatoye et al., 2024).

Democratic Leadership: This approach encourages collaboration, boosting job satisfaction and morale. However, it may be time-consuming and less effective in urgent situations (Kiwanuka et al., 2021).

Laissez-faire Leadership: Laissez-faire leadership offers autonomy, fostering creativity and innovation, but may result in a lack of direction and coordination (Bwalya, 2023).

Adaptive Leadership: Adaptive leadership helps healthcare organizations navigate uncertainty and change by fostering a learning culture. However, continuous adaptation can overwhelm organizations if not managed effectively (Olatoye et al., 2024).

Situational Leadership: This style allows leaders to adapt their approach based on the situation and team readiness. Misapplication or inconsistent execution may confuse (Olatoye et al., 2024).

4.3 Emotional Intelligence and Leadership Styles

A study by k Kasemaa and Vadi (2023) examines the relationship between healthcare managers' leadership behaviors, emotional intelligence (EI), and healthcare workers' perceptions in an Estonian hospital. It finds that transformational and transactional leadership behaviors positively impact job satisfaction and commitment, enhancing patient care quality. Emotional intelligence significantly influences leadership effectiveness, with reward behaviors positively linked to EI and punishment behaviors negatively linked.

The research highlights the importance of understanding employee diversity (e.g., gender, nationality, qualifications, tenure) to optimize leadership strategies. It recommends integrating EI training into leadership development programs and suggests using the cut version of the Genos Emotional Intelligence Inventory for healthcare leadership research in Estonia.

4.4 Implications of Leadership Styles

The research underscores that emotional intelligence enhances both leadership styles, enabling healthcare managers to adapt their approach to employee needs and workplace diversity.

Transformational leadership benefits most from EI, requiring empathy, inspiration, and individualized support. Meanwhile, transactional leaders with high EI can better balance rewards and constructive feedback to achieve organizational goals.

This insight reinforces the need to integrate EI training into leadership development programs for healthcare managers to optimize leadership styles and improve outcomes.

4.5 Types of Followers in Healthcare

To understand leadership practically, it is advisable to dissect the concept into three main pillars: leader, followers, and context. This helps us understand different leadership situations. Understanding each pillar's different states and combinations of these states will also help us better ourselves as leaders.

Depending on different contexts, a leader can assume different leadership styles with the same team. For example, being democratic with a team in a specific context does not prevent the same leader from assuming an autocratic style in a different context, such as in emergencies.

Therefore, leaders should invest time and effort into understanding different styles and when to use each. Also, understanding your followers is of paramount importance. People, and hence the workforce you work with as a leader, are the main initiators of nearly every activity inside the organization. Understanding different personalities around you and their different profiles under various conditions is worth it.

Third, there is context. Different contexts might mandate different leadership styles even with the same team. Therefore, an effective leader should be self-conscious of, at least, the most everyday contexts encountered in the business environment.

To summarize, leaders, followers, and context are the main three predictors of organizational leadership outcomes. This could be mathematical represented as:

$$Y \text{ (leadership outcome)} \approx A \text{ (Leader style)} + B \text{ (Followers)} + C \text{ (Context)}$$

In the previous section, we discussed different leadership styles; in this section, we will display different categories encountered in healthcare, followed by different contexts in the following section.

Common categories of followers in healthcare are:

· Physicians

Independent decision-makers with specialized expertise.

The physician's role in a changing healthcare system is multifaceted, requiring adaptability to technological advancements, evolving patient expectations, and shifts in healthcare delivery. Physicians are not only caregivers but also collaborators within interdisciplinary teams, ensuring holistic care that meets the diverse needs of patients. They must navigate complex systems, balancing clinical responsibilities with ethical considerations and resource management. Physicians are called to embrace flexibility, engage in continuous learning, and align their practices with emerging trends to enhance patient outcomes and system efficiency as healthcare transforms. Their role is pivotal in driving quality care while fostering patient trust and communication.

Here are the key roles of physicians in a changing healthcare system:

1. **Patient Care:** Diagnosing and treating illnesses, managing health, and ensuring comprehensive care.

2. **Advocate:** Acting as a patient advocate, ensuring access to appropriate treatments and resources.

3. **Team Leader:** Collaborating with healthcare teams to provide integrated, multidisciplinary care.

4. **Educator:** Educating patients about their conditions, treatments, and preventive health measures.

5. **Researcher:** Contributing to medical research and staying updated on the latest advancements and practices.

6. **Ethical Decision-Maker:** Upholding ethical standards and addressing complex medical and moral issues.

7. **Communicator:** Building trust through effective communication with patients and families.

8. **Public Health Advocate:** Participating in community health initiatives and advocating for public health improvements.

9. **Lifelong Learner:** Continuously updating skills and knowledge to stay current with medical advancements.

10. **Policy Contributor:** Shaping healthcare policies and improving system-level processes.

https://www.ncbi.nlm.nih.gov/books/NBK217690/

· Nurses

Collaborative team members focusing on patient care.

The nursing profession plays a vital role in improving healthcare quality by providing patient care, administering treatments, and supporting the diagnostic and therapeutic processes led by doctors. Nurses are essential members of healthcare teams, engaging in tasks such as assessing patient needs, planning care, and performing health promotion activities. They also contribute to research, manage nursing teams, and provide health education.

Nursing is evolving to meet growing patient expectations and incorporates continuous professional development. The profession focuses on holistic care, addressing biological, psychological, and social health factors. Nurses' contributions significantly influence patient satisfaction, safety, and trust, making them critical to healthcare institutions' success.

Key activities of nurses include:

- Recognizing and addressing patient needs.

- Plan and deliver care autonomously or in collaboration with other professionals.

- Promoting prevention and health education.

- Participating in research and health policy formulation.

- Engaging in ongoing professional training.

The profession's development aligns with societal health needs, emphasizing the dynamic nature of health and the increasing demand for quality care.

· Allied Healthcare Professionals

The role of allied health care professionals in end-of-life care extends beyond their traditional rehabilitation responsibilities, encompassing critical support in medical decision-making and advance care planning. Professionals such as speech-language pathologists and occupational therapists are vital in guiding patients through complex end-of-life choices. Their trusted relationships with patients enable them to understand and respect individual values and beliefs, facilitating meaningful communication during this sensitive time.

Key responsibilities include:

- Assisting in the preparation of advance directives and care plans.

- Providing education on medical decision-making and informed consent.

- Navigating legal and policy considerations related to advance care planning.

- Utilizing decision-making models and motivational interviewing tools to support patient autonomy.

- Advocating for the patient during the implementation of advanced care plans, especially when the patient becomes incapable of making decisions.

• Administrative Staff

Key supporters of operational efficiency and organizational goals.

Research by Dr. Godwin Ayittey (2023) explores the critical role of hospital administrators in ensuring healthcare excellence. The study highlights their multifaceted responsibilities, including strategic planning, fiscal management, regulatory compliance, and staff oversight. A mixed-method approach emphasizes how administrators impact patient care, organizational efficiency, and the overall healthcare environment.

Key responsibilities include:

1. **Strategic Planning:** Developing long-term plans that adapt to industry changes and align with the hospital's goals.

2. **Financial Management:** Overseeing budgeting, cost control, resource allocation, and revenue generation.

3. **Human Resources Management:** Managing recruitment, training, employee relations, and performance to ensure quality care.

4. **Emergency Preparedness:** Planning for crises, ensuring patient safety, and coordinating with external agencies.

5. **Public Health Initiatives:** Supporting community health, education, and collaboration with public health agencies.

The research underscores the importance of administrators' adaptability, leadership, and proactive approach in navigating challenges like technological advancements and evolving regulations, ultimately contributing to sustaining healthcare excellence.

Chapter 5: The Role of Context in Leadership Effectiveness

5.1 The nature of the healthcare context

The healthcare context is uniquely complex, setting it apart from other industries and its past. Unlike more linear or predictable environments, healthcare operates within a dynamic and high-stakes ecosystem characterized by rapidly evolving technology, regulatory constraints, diverse patient needs, and interdisciplinary collaboration. This complexity demands adaptive leadership styles that navigate uncertainty, prioritize ethical decision-making, and foster collaboration across varied teams.
Transformational leadership, for instance, becomes essential to inspire innovation and drive change, while situational leadership is critical to responding to fluctuating demands. The intricate nature of healthcare also necessitates emotionally intelligent leaders who can balance operational efficiency with empathy, ensuring both organizational goals and patient outcomes are achieved. In such a multifaceted environment, effective leadership hinges on understanding and adapting to the unique challenges of the healthcare context.

5.2 The impact of Healthcare context on leadership styles

In healthcare, the complexity and unpredictability of the context require leaders to adopt flexible and context-specific leadership styles. Transformational leadership is often effective, inspiring teams to embrace innovation and adapt to rapid advancements in medical technology and patient care practices. Situational leadership is equally vital, enabling leaders to adjust their approach based on the immediate needs of their team or organization, whether addressing a crisis, implementing new policies, or guiding long-term change. Servant leadership also aligns well with healthcare, emphasizing empathy, collaboration, and a commitment to serving patients and team members. By aligning leadership style with the

demands of the healthcare context, leaders can foster resilience, enhance teamwork, and ensure that organizational goals are achieved without compromising the quality of care.

5.3 Quick Check 

1. What is the primary focus of Transactional Leadership?

a) Building personal relationships and inspiring followers

b) Establishing rules, expectations, and rewards for performance

c) Adapting leadership style based on follower needs

d) Encouraging creativity and innovation

2. Which of the following is an essential characteristic of Democratic Leadership?

a) Leaders make decisions without consulting followers

b) Leaders focus primarily on task completion and performance metrics

c) Leaders encourage group decision-making and participation

d) Leaders centralize decision-making to maintain control

3. Which of the following situations is Autocratic Leadership most effective in?

a) When followers are highly experienced and capable

b) In a crisis or emergency requiring quick decisions

c) When leaders want to develop a team-oriented culture

d) In environments that encourage creative problem-solving

4. Which leadership theory emphasizes the leader's ability to understand and manage their emotions and those of their followers?

a) Path-Goal Theory

b) Emotional Intelligence

c) Situational Leadership

d) Transformational Leadership

5. In the context of leadership, what does the Contingency Theory suggest?

a) Leaders are born with inherent traits that determine their success

b) Leadership effectiveness depends on the fit between the leader's style and the situation

c) Leadership should focus solely on followers' needs

d) Leaders should never adapt their style to the situation

Correct answers:

1- B

2- C

3- B

4- B

5- B

5.4 Case Study: The Role of Leadership in a Crisis at a Rural Health Clinic

Background: A rural health clinic has been struggling with limited resources, high patient volume, and a shortage of medical staff. A significant crisis occurs when an unexpected contagious disease outbreak strains the clinic's capacity to provide adequate care. The clinic's director, Sarah Thompson, must make critical decisions under pressure while managing a small, highly stressed team.

Sarah's predominantly democratic leadership style has helped her build strong relationships with her staff and encourage their involvement in decision-making. However, due to the rapid increase in patients and the situation's complexity, the clinic cannot operate at its usual pace in this crisis.

Sarah needs to quickly adjust her leadership approach to address the urgent needs of the clinic while maintaining morale and cohesion within her team. She temporarily shifts to a Transactional Leadership style, setting clear guidelines for team members, establishing performance metrics, and offering rewards for meeting specific targets in managing the outbreak.

Despite the urgency, Sarah struggles with maintaining her typically collaborative approach in such a high-pressure environment. Some staff members feel overwhelmed by the new structure and unclear expectations.

1. How does Sarah's Democratic Leadership style influence her ability to respond to the crisis, and what are the benefits and challenges of this approach in a high-pressure situation?

2. What are the advantages of Sarah shifting to Transactional Leadership during the crisis? How could this help improve the clinic's response to the outbreak?

3. Given the rural clinic's context, would an Autocratic Leadership style be more effective during the crisis? Why or why not?

4. How does Emotional Intelligence affect Sarah's leadership effectiveness in crisis management? What strategies could she use to maintain team morale while addressing the clinic's immediate needs?

5. How can Sarah balance her Democratic leadership style with the more directive aspects of Transactional Leadership to ensure both immediate crisis management and long-term team development?

Chapter 6: Power in Leadership

6.1 Introduction: The Concept of Power in Healthcare

Power is a fundamental aspect of leadership that shapes how decisions are made, actions are taken, and relationships are managed within healthcare organizations. In healthcare leadership, power dynamics are particularly unique due to hierarchical structures and the need for interdisciplinary collaboration. Leaders must understand these dynamics to influence effectively, navigate complex environments, and ensure equitable decision-making that prioritizes patient care.

6.2 Types of Power

1. Legitimate Power: Authority from Position

o Stemming from a leader's official role or title, this type of power grants authority to set policies, make decisions, and direct team activities.

2. Expert Power: Knowledge and Skill-Based Influence

o Derived from a leader's expertise and specialized knowledge, this power fosters trust and confidence among team members.

3. Referent Power: Charismatic and Relational Influence

o Built on personal relationships, respect, and admiration, referent power enables leaders to motivate and inspire teams through connection and trust.

4. Reward Power: Incentive-Based Authority

o Leveraging the ability to provide rewards, such as promotions, recognition, or incentives, leaders can drive motivation and achieve desired behaviors.

5. Coercive Power: Influence Through Discipline or Threat

o Although less ideal, coercive power involves using threats or disciplinary actions to enforce compliance, needing careful ethical considerations.

6.3 Sources of Power in Healthcare Organizations

1. Professional Expertise and Credentials

o Leaders with advanced knowledge, clinical expertise, or specialized skills gain credibility and influence within healthcare settings.

2. Institutional Policies and Decision-Making Authority

o Power derived from organizational structures and governance frameworks enables leaders to shape healthcare policies and procedures.

3. Interpersonal Relationships and Networks

o Building strong professional networks and fostering relationships across departments amplifies a leader's ability to influence and collaborate.

6.4 Ethical Use of Power in Leadership

1. Promoting Transparency and Integrity

o Leaders should use power to build trust by maintaining open communication and aligning actions with ethical principles.

2. Avoiding Abuse of Authority

o Ensuring decisions and actions are inclusive, fair, and in the best interest of patients and staff.

6.5 The impact of power on health care team performance and patient safety

This refers to how power dynamics within healthcare teams influence their ability to communicate, collaborate, make decisions, and ultimately deliver safe and effective patient care. When power imbalances exist due to hierarchy, authority, or perceived status, they can hinder teamwork, leading to poor communication, less effective decision-making, and reduced team performance. This, in turn, can increase the risk of patient harm or safety issues.

For example, when lower-ranking team members feel unable to speak up due to a dominant or authoritative figure, significant concerns may not be addressed, leading to errors or missed opportunities for better patient care. On the other hand, an environment where power is more equally distributed tends to foster better collaboration, decision-making, and safer outcomes for patients.

A review article by Stevens, Hulme, & Salmon (2021) explores how power dynamics within healthcare teams affect communication, collaboration, decision-making, and patient safety. Despite extensive research on teamwork in healthcare, the influence of power on outcomes like patient safety and team performance has been underexplored. The review, which assessed 19 studies, found that power imbalances often negatively impact teamwork. These findings suggest that further research is needed in the ergonomics field better to understand the role of power in healthcare settings and to improve patient safety and team performance.

The article further elaborates on the key findings of the literature review regarding the role of power within multidisciplinary healthcare teams. The studies reviewed suggest that power imbalances, whether real or perceived, can have detrimental effects on various aspects of team functioning. Specifically, power dynamics can lead to poor communication, hinder collaboration, affect decision-making, and negatively impact overall team performance. These issues are linked to increased risks to patient safety.

The authors highlight the need for further research, particularly in ergonomics, to examine the complex relationship between power and teamwork in healthcare. Understanding this interplay could improve strategies for fostering better team dynamics and enhancing patient care and safety outcomes. The review calls for more focused studies, emphasizing the importance of addressing power-related challenges in healthcare settings to optimize team performance and reduce errors.

Additionally, the review introduces several terms and frameworks, such as Crew Resource Management (CRM), Threat and Error Management (TEM), and Social Network Analysis (SNA), which are often applied in understanding teamwork in high-stakes environments like healthcare.

6.6 Power dynamics in healthcare teams – a barrier to team effectiveness and patient safety

Kearns et al. (2021) found that power dynamics within healthcare teams hinder team effectiveness and patient safety. Key points likely covered in the study include:

- **Impact of Hierarchies:** Hierarchical structures in healthcare teams often lead to uneven power distribution, where junior staff or less authoritative team members feel less confident about voicing concerns or contributing to decision-making.

- **Communication Barriers:** Unequal power dynamics hinder open communication, as team members in lower positions may fear retaliation or dismissal of their input, which can lead to overlooking critical information.

- **Patient Safety Risks:** The inability to address power imbalances can lead to errors, as staff may avoid reporting mistakes or safety issues, fearing blame or punitive actions.

- **Collaboration Challenges:** Power imbalances disrupt team cohesion and interprofessional collaboration, reducing the ability to work effectively as a unit.

6.7 Strategies to Balance Power Dynamics

1. Fostering Psychological Safety

Encouraging an environment where team members feel safe to express concerns, ask questions, and share ideas without fear of judgment or retribution. Psychological safety helps overcome hierarchical barriers and ensures critical information is shared.

Implementation: Regular debriefings, anonymous feedback channels, and leader behaviors that promote openness and inclusivity.

Example: Leaders acknowledging their own mistakes to model vulnerability and trust.

2. Promoting Interprofessional Collaboration

Developing structured collaboration frameworks that encourage all team members to contribute equitably, regardless of rank or role.

Implementation: Utilizing interprofessional education programs, joint training sessions, and collaborative decision-making tools.

Example: Including all relevant disciplines in care planning meetings to ensure comprehensive perspectives.

3. Adopting Flat Hierarchies

Reducing rigid hierarchies within teams to create a more egalitarian structure where all voices are valued.

Implementation: Establish team norms prioritizing expertise and input over rank during discussions or decision-making processes.

Example: Using role rotation in team leadership to allow everyone to lead and learn.

4. Encouraging Open Communication

Implementing structured communication tools ensures all team members can effectively contribute and escalate concerns.

Implementation: Utilizing models like SBAR (Situation-Background-Assessment-Recommendation) to standardize communication across hierarchies.

Example: Mandatory rounds where each team member, including junior staff, could present observations or recommendations.

5. Training in Conflict Resolution and Power Awareness

Providing education on managing conflicts and understanding the impact of power dynamics in healthcare teams.

Implementation: Training sessions that teach negotiation, mediation, and interest-based problem-solving.

Example: Workshops focused on recognizing and addressing implicit biases tied to professional hierarchies.

6. Implementing Shared Governance Models

Establishing governance structures that distribute authority across team members, empowering them to make decisions collectively.

Implementation: Creating councils or committees where team members from various levels have equal representation.

Example: Nurse-led councils that have decision-making authority over policies affecting clinical workflows.

7. Providing Leadership Development

Ensuring leaders understand the importance of equitable team dynamics and learn skills to manage power constructively.

Implementation: Leadership training programs focusing on emotional intelligence, active listening, and inclusive leadership styles.

Example: Coaching senior leaders to prioritize input from all team members during decision-making processes.

8. Setting up Clear Reporting Structures

Creating systems for reporting power misuse or communication failures without fear of reprisal.

Implementation: Anonymous reporting platforms and clear escalation protocols for concerns related to power imbalances.

Example: A confidential system for junior staff to report concerns directly to neutral mediators or patient safety officers.

9. Enhancing Team Accountability

Shifting focus from individual blame to team-based accountability for errors and outcomes.

Implementation: Using root-cause analysis during adverse events to identify system-wide solutions rather than focusing on individual faults.

Example: Blame-free culture initiatives where learning is emphasized over punishment.

6.8 Quick Check

1. What is an example of Legitimate Power in healthcare leadership?

a) A leader's ability to provide incentives or rewards

b) A leader's authority derived from their official position in the organization

c) A leader's influence due to their relationships and respect from others

d) A leader's power is based on their specialized expertise and knowledge

2. What type of power is based on a leader's specialized knowledge or expertise within healthcare?

a) Expert Power

b) Coercive Power

c) Reward Power

d) Legitimate Power

3. Which of the following is key in promoting psychological safety in healthcare teams?

a) Leaders making all decisions without input from others

b) Team members feeling safe to express concerns without fear of judgment or retribution

c) Maintaining a rigid hierarchical structure in decision-making

d) Only senior leaders are involved in discussions about patient safety

4. According to the review by Stevens, Hulme, and Salmon (2021), power imbalances in healthcare teams often lead to:

a) Increased patient satisfaction

b) better decision-making and communication

c) Poor communication, reduced collaboration, and higher patient safety risks

d) Improved team performance and morale

5. What is one strategy to balance power dynamics and enhance team effectiveness in healthcare?

a) Avoiding conflict resolution and focusing on hierarchical authority

b) Implementing flat hierarchies and promoting interprofessional collaboration

c) Restricting communication to senior staff only

d) Encouraging one leader to make all decisions independently

Correct answers

1 - B

2 - A

3 - B

4 - C

5 - B

6.9 Case Study: Patient-Centred Care at Riverside Health System

Riverside Health System implemented a patient engagement strategy to improve communication and foster a more personalized care experience. The initiative included setting up patient advisory councils, creating customized care plans, and implementing a patient portal for easier access to medical records and communication with healthcare providers. They also integrated mobile health apps to remind patients of upcoming appointments and treatments.

Discussion Questions:

How did Riverside Health System improve patient engagement through personalized care plans and portals?

What impact did mobile health apps have on patient engagement and treatment adherence?

What challenges did the healthcare system face in implementing these strategies, and how were they addressed?

How can healthcare leaders encourage greater patient involvement in their care?

Chapter 7: Communication and Collaboration

7.1 Effective Communication Strategies in Healthcare

Effective communication is vital for ensuring the success of healthcare teams, enhancing patient safety, and improving clinical outcomes. Healthcare leaders must employ diverse strategies to bridge communication gaps and foster a culture of clarity, understanding, and collaboration across professional boundaries.

1. Active Listening and Clear Messaging Techniques

Active listening and clear messaging are fundamental to effective communication in healthcare. Active listening involves fully concentrating, understanding, responding, and remembering what the other person is saying (Brownell, 2012). Leaders in healthcare settings must be adept at listening attentively to their teams and patients and demonstrating empathy and concern, which improves trust and collaboration.

To ensure clarity, leaders must paraphrase statements to confirm understanding, eliminating potential confusion. Additionally, concise and precise language is critical in avoiding misunderstandings, especially when conveying complex medical information (Baker et al., 2017). Active listening promotes interpersonal respect and helps with problem-solving and effective decision-making. By reducing the occurrence of miscommunication, healthcare teams can function more efficiently and provide higher-quality care to patients.

2. Addressing Communication Barriers in Diverse Teams

Healthcare teams often consist of professionals from diverse backgrounds, and communication barriers can arise due to language differences, cultural nuances, and hierarchical pressures (Van de Bovenkamp et al., 2020). Language barriers are particularly prevalent in multicultural healthcare settings, where team members and patients may speak different languages. Misunderstandings can lead to errors, reduced patient satisfaction, and fragmented care.

Cultural competency and sensitivity to cultural nuances are essential for overcoming these barriers (Betancourt et al., 2003). Training staff in cultural competence helps them understand different patient populations' specific communication needs and preferences, promoting more effective interactions. Additionally, recognizing and addressing hierarchical pressures within healthcare teams is crucial. Lower-ranking staff may hesitate to speak up in the presence of higher-ranking professionals, inhibiting open communication.

Leaders must foster an environment where everyone feels empowered to contribute, regardless of rank or background.

Chapter 8: Leading Interdisciplinary Teams

Interdisciplinary teamwork is a hallmark of high-functioning healthcare settings. Effective leaders are pivotal in fostering collaboration, ensuring that diverse professional perspectives contribute to patient care. Working in a team is common in healthcare. This is nearly the norm, as patient care seldom depends on a single professional effort. Consequently, healthcare leaders should be able to lead multidisciplinary teams with different skills, backgrounds, and attitudes.

8.1 Setting up Common Goals and Fostering Unity

To improve team performance, healthcare leaders must set common goals that align the efforts of diverse team members.

Establishing shared goals helps healthcare professionals from different disciplines (e.g., doctors, nurses, social workers, and therapists) work together toward a unified purpose (O'Daniel & Rosenstein, 2008). This approach reduces fragmentation in care delivery, encourages cooperation, and enhances team cohesion. By creating clear, measurable goals that everyone in the team can agree upon, leaders ensure that each member's contribution is valued and that all members are working towards the same endpoint, enhancing the quality of patient care.

8.2 Recognizing and Leveraging Team Members' Strengths

A leader's ability to recognize the strengths and expertise of individual team members is crucial for maximizing team performance (Tannenbaum et al., 2012). In healthcare settings, recognizing and assigning roles based on individuals' skills and experiences leads to more efficient and effective team functioning. For example, a nurse with expertise in patient education might lead patient counseling, while a physician specializing in cardiology takes the lead on heart-related treatments. Leaders increase team members' satisfaction and improve clinical outcomes by aligning team tasks with personal strengths.

Chapter 9: Conflict Resolution and Problem Solving

Healthcare teams are often under high pressure, which can lead to conflicts. Effective leaders must implement strategies to manage and resolve these conflicts while ensuring the team's continued efficiency and patient safety.

9.1 Techniques for De-escalating Conflicts

Conflict in healthcare teams can arise due to differences in opinion, stress, or misunderstandings. Effective leaders use conflict resolution strategies such as mediation, active listening, and reframing to reduce tensions (Kreps, 2014). Active listening in conflict situations allows individuals to feel heard, promoting a sense of respect and reducing hostility. Reframing is another powerful tool that helps shift the focus from blame or personal attacks to resolving the issue. Leaders can de-escalate tensions and maintain team harmony by focusing on the underlying problems rather than interpersonal conflicts.

9.2 Collaborative Approaches to Finding Solutions

When conflict arises, involving the entire team in problem-solving is essential to reach a consensus. Collaborative approaches ensure that every voice is heard and that solutions benefit from the diverse perspectives within the team (Schroeder et al., 2018). Facilitating joint problem-solving sessions allows team members to brainstorm solutions, build consensus, and agree on a course of action. This collective effort addresses the conflict, strengthens team cohesion, and promotes a shared commitment to resolving issues in patient care.

9.3 Quick Check

1. What is the primary goal of active listening in healthcare settings?

a) To respond quickly without waiting for the speaker to finish
b) To fully understand and remember the message being communicated
c) To agree with the speaker's point of view
d) To interrupt the speaker with clarifications

2. Which of the following is a key strategy to address communication barriers in diverse healthcare teams?

a) Speaking more slowly to all team members

b) Providing standardized communication training
c) Relying on technology to bridge language gaps
d) Encouraging the use of medical jargon for efficiency

3. What should healthcare leaders focus on to improve collaboration in interdisciplinary teams?

a) Ensuring that each professional works independently
b) Creating common goals and fostering unity among team members
c) Allowing team members to only work within their departments
d) Emphasizing competition among team members

4. Which approach is most effective for resolving conflict in healthcare teams?

a) Avoiding the conflict until it resolves itself
b) Reframing the conflict to focus on underlying issues rather than personal differences
c) Taking sides and supporting one team member over another
d) Ignoring the conflict and focusing on patient care

5. What is the benefit of fostering collaboration in healthcare teams?

a) Increased isolation among team members
b) Better decision-making and improved patient care
c) Less need for communication
d) Reduced trust among team members

Correct answers

1- B

2- B

3- B

4- B

5- B

9.4 Case Study: Ethical Dilemma at Green Valley Hospital

Green Valley Hospital faced a problematic ethical decision when a pharmaceutical company offered a large donation in exchange for exclusive rights to distribute its drugs within the hospital. While the donation would provide significant funding, hospital leadership had to weigh the potential conflicts of interest and the risks of prioritizing profit over patient welfare. The leadership team engaged in discussions, consulted with ethics committees, and rejected donations to maintain their commitment to patient-centered care.

Discussion Questions:

1. What ethical principles did Green Valley Hospital need to consider when considering the donation offer?

2. How did the hospital leadership show ethical decision-making in this scenario?

3. What impact could accepting the donation have had on the hospital's reputation and patient trust?

4. How can healthcare leaders prioritize ethical considerations in decision-making processes?

Chapter 10: Decision-Making and Strategic Thinking

Effective decision-making and strategic thinking are critical skills for healthcare leaders. With rapidly changing healthcare environments, leaders must make informed decisions that balance clinical needs, operational goals, and patient care outcomes. This module delves into evidence-based decision-making, balancing patient needs with organizational goals, risk management strategies, and creating and executing strategic plans. Leaders have the tools to make well-informed decisions and drive long-term organizational success.

10.1 Evidence-Based Decision-Making

In healthcare, decisions must be driven by the best available evidence to ensure the highest quality of care. Evidence-based decision-making (EBDM) involves integrating clinical expertise with the best research evidence and patient preferences. This process ensures that healthcare leaders make well-informed decisions that lead to better outcomes and enhance operational efficiency.

- **Using Clinical Data and Best Practices to Guide Decisions**

» Evidence-based decision-making relies on clinical data and best practices to guide healthcare decisions. Leaders must ensure that healthcare providers have access to reliable data sources and can interpret these data effectively. By using clinical guidelines and research evidence, healthcare leaders can make informed decisions that are scientifically grounded, leading to improved patient outcomes. This approach reduces variations in care and minimizes the risk of errors, thus enhancing overall healthcare quality.

- **Balancing Patient Needs with Organizational Goals**

» Healthcare leaders must balance individual patient care needs with organizational goals such as efficiency, cost-effectiveness, and resource management. This can be challenging, especially when patient care decisions conflict with budget constraints or organizational priorities. For example, a leader may need to decide between a treatment that best serves the patient's needs and one that is more cost-effective or better aligned with available resources. Effective decision-making requires a delicate balance, considering clinical needs and organizational constraints. Leaders can make decisions that benefit patients and the organization by fostering a culture that values patient-centered care and operational efficiency.

10.2 Risk Management in Leadership

Risk management is a vital component of healthcare leadership. Healthcare leaders must proactively identify potential risks and take steps to mitigate them. Risk management includes clinical, financial, and operational risks impacting patient safety, organizational performance, and regulation compliance. Leaders must also prepare their teams to handle crises and maintain stability during uncertain times.

- **Identifying and Mitigating Potential Risks**

» Healthcare leaders must develop a thorough understanding of the risks that their organizations face. This includes clinical risks such as adverse events and medical errors and operational and financial risks like budget deficits or staffing shortages. Leaders must employ risk assessments, audits, and monitoring systems to identify potential risks early. Proactive mitigation strategies could involve developing contingency plans, investing in staff training, or improving communication channels. By identifying and addressing risks before they escalate, leaders can prevent significant challenges and ensure a safe environment for patients and healthcare workers.

- **Leading Teams Through Uncertainty**

» Healthcare leaders often manage teams through times of uncertainty, such as during a crisis, organizational restructuring, or significant changes in healthcare policy. Effective leadership during uncertain times requires effective communication, decision-making, and emotional intelligence. Leaders must reassure their teams, provide clarity, and confidently make decisions, even when the outcomes are unclear. By maintaining team morale, fostering a supportive environment, and ensuring transparent communication, leaders can guide their teams through periods of uncertainty and prevent burnout or disengagement.

10.3 Creating and Executing Strategic Plans

Strategic planning is a vital process for healthcare leaders. It provides a clear roadmap for achieving organizational goals and ensuring long-term success. Effective strategic planning requires leaders to set realistic goals, allocate resources effectively, and adapt to changing circumstances. Healthcare leaders must also be able to monitor progress, evaluate outcomes, and make necessary adjustments to stay on course.

- **Steps for Effective Strategic Planning**

» Effective strategic planning begins with a thorough assessment of the current situation. This involves analyzing internal strengths and weaknesses and external opportunities and threats (SWOT analysis). This assessment allows leaders to set clear, measurable goals aligned with the organization's mission and vision. To meet these objectives, They must efficiently allocate resources—such as finances, personnel, and time. Leaders should involve key stakeholders, including clinical staff, patients, and external partners, in the strategic planning process to ensure buy-in and shared goals. Additionally, strategic plans should include timelines and performance metrics to ensure accountability.

- **Monitoring and Adapting Plans as Needed**

» While strategic plans provide direction, healthcare leaders must remain flexible and responsive to changes in the healthcare environment. This includes external changes such as policy reforms, technological advancements, market shifts, and internal changes like staffing fluctuations or new patient care needs. Leaders should establish systems for monitoring progress, gathering feedback, and evaluating performance against established goals. Leaders should be prepared to adapt their plans based on real-time data, emerging challenges, or new opportunities when necessary. Continuous evaluation and adaptation ensure the organization stays on track toward its long-term goals.

10.4 Quick Check

1. Evidence-based decision-making (EBDM) in healthcare involves integrating which of the following?

a) financial data with patient preferences
b) Clinical expertise with the best research evidence and patient preferences
c) Patient preferences with organizational goals
d) Only the best research evidence with clinical expertise

2. How can healthcare leaders balance patient care needs with organizational goals?

a) By always prioritizing patient care over organizational constraints
b) By fostering a culture that values both patient-centered care and operational efficiency
c) By cutting costs to focus solely on patient needs
d) By ignoring organizational constraints and focusing only on individual treatments

3. What is a key strategy in risk management for healthcare leaders?

a) Reacting only when a risk becomes evident
b) Identifying and mitigating potential risks proactively
c) Ignoring minor risks and focusing on major ones
d) Relying solely on insurance policies to manage risks

4. What should healthcare leaders do when navigating uncertainty in their organizations?

a) Avoid making decisions until all risks are clear
b) Communicate clearly, make decisions confidently, and support their teams emotionally
c) Allow uncertainty to dictate the team's actions without direction
d) Avoid communicating with the team about the uncertainty

5. What is the first step in creating an effective strategic plan for a healthcare organization?

a) Analysing internal strengths and weaknesses
b) Setting financial goals
c) Allocating resources
d) Focusing on patient care outcomes

Correct answers:

1- B

2- B

3- B

4- B

5- A

10.5 Case Study: Budget Cuts at Metro Medical Centre

Metro Medical Centre, a large urban hospital, faced significant budget cuts due to a reduction in government funding. The hospital leadership team had to make complex decisions to maintain high-quality care while managing costs. They implemented financial strategies, including renegotiating supplier contracts, reducing administrative overhead, and optimizing resource utilization. These efforts helped Metro Medical Centre achieve a 15% reduction in operational costs while maintaining patient satisfaction and care quality.

Discussion Questions:

1. What financial strategies did Metro Medical Centre employ to reduce operational costs while maintaining care quality?

2. How can healthcare leaders balance financial sustainability with the need for high-quality patient care?

3. What role does fiscal management play in the overall success of healthcare organizations?

4. What challenges did the leadership team face in implementing cost-saving measures without compromising patient outcomes?

Chapter 11: Being an Effective Leader in Healthcare

Effective healthcare leadership requires a multifaceted approach. The healthcare environment is complex and involves a variety of stakeholders, from patients and healthcare providers to regulatory bodies and external partners. Healthcare leaders must be adept at navigating these complexities and fostering an environment of trust, engagement, and collaboration. This module explores key strategies for leading effectively in the healthcare sector, building confidence, engaging stakeholders, promoting a patient-centered culture, and leveraging technology.

11.1 Building Trust and Credibility as a Leader

Trust is the cornerstone of effective leadership in healthcare. Healthcare professionals must trust their leaders to make decisions that prioritize patient care, support staff well-being, and navigate organizational challenges. Building trust begins with demonstrating honesty, integrity, and transparency in decision-making and communication.

11.2 Honesty and Integrity

Leaders must lead by example, displaying the highest standards of honesty and integrity in all interactions. This involves being transparent about organizational goals, challenges, and decisions. For instance, when introducing new policies or changes, leaders should communicate the rationale behind the decisions and how they align with the organization's mission and vision. When staff members see leaders acting with integrity, they are likelier to adopt similar behaviors, fostering a culture of trust throughout the organization.

11.3 Building Reliability and Accountability

Healthcare leaders must consistently meet expectations and deliver on promises to build credibility. This requires leaders to demonstrate competence, reliability, and accountability. By setting clear expectations and holding themselves and others accountable, leaders can create a stable, dependable work environment where staff feel confident in their leadership. Leaders must also be willing to admit mistakes and take responsibility when things go wrong, further enhancing their credibility.

11.4 Engaging Stakeholders in Healthcare Decision-Making

Effective healthcare leadership involves engaging a wide range of stakeholders in decision-making processes. These include clinical staff, patients, their families, policymakers, and the broader community. Engaging stakeholders fosters a sense of ownership and ensures that diverse perspectives are considered when making critical decisions.

1. Involving Patients in Decision-Making

Patient-centered care is at the heart of modern healthcare. Leaders must find ways to engage patients in the decision-making process, ensuring that their preferences and values are considered in care plans. This could involve shared decision-making models where healthcare providers collaborate with patients to discuss treatment options and outcomes. By involving patients in their care decisions, leaders can enhance patient satisfaction, improve adherence to treatment plans, and ultimately improve outcomes.

2. Engaging Healthcare Staff and External Partners

In addition to patients, leaders must engage their healthcare teams and external partners in decision-making. This requires creating an inclusive environment where all voices are heard, whether from medical professionals, administrative staff, or external collaborators such as insurance companies and regulatory bodies. Leaders can foster engagement by encouraging open communication, soliciting feedback, and promoting cross-disciplinary collaboration. Engaging staff and external partners ensures that decisions are informed by diverse expertise and perspectives, leading to more comprehensive, well-rounded outcomes.

11.5 Promoting a Patient-Centred Culture

A patient-centered approach to healthcare leadership is essential for improving patient outcomes and organizational performance. Leaders must create an environment where patient's needs and preferences are prioritized, and patient care is delivered compassionately, respectfully, and culturally sensitively.

1. Aligning Leadership Practices with Patient Care Goals

To promote a patient-centered culture, leaders must align organizational practices to deliver the highest quality care to patients. This includes ensuring that healthcare teams are trained to provide compassionate, holistic care that considers patients' physical, emotional, and social needs. Leaders should also ensure that resources are allocated to support patient-centered initiatives, such as patient education, advocacy, and personalized care plans.

2. Creating an Organizational Culture that Supports Patient-Centred Care

Beyond individual leadership practices, healthcare leaders must foster an organizational culture that supports patient-centered care. This includes creating policies and systems prioritizing patient well-being and ensuring that all healthcare providers are committed to delivering high-quality care. Leaders should also encourage staff to engage in continuous professional development and to be proactive in identifying and addressing barriers to patient-centered care.

11.6 Quick Check

1. What is one of the key components of building trust as a healthcare leader?

a) Avoiding transparency to protect staff from lousy news
b) Demonstrating honesty, integrity, and transparency in decision-making
c) Using authority to control all decisions
d) Keeping decisions and communication private from the team

2. How can healthcare leaders effectively engage stakeholders in decision-making?

a) By only involving senior medical staff in the decision-making process
b) By engaging all stakeholders, including patients, families, and external partners
c) By making all decisions unilaterally without consulting others
d) By focusing only on clinical staff input

3. How can a leader promote a patient-centered culture in healthcare?

a) By focusing solely on the efficiency of the healthcare system
b) By aligning organizational practices to deliver the highest quality care to patients
c) By reducing patient involvement in decision-making
d) By prioritizing operational goals over patient care

4. What is an essential characteristic for a healthcare leader to demonstrate to build credibility?

a) Keeping personal goals private
b) Consistently meeting expectations and being reliable
c) Delegating all decision-making to others
d) Avoiding responsibility when things go wrong

5. What should a healthcare leader do to encourage collaboration among team members?

a) Force all staff to follow a strict hierarchy
b) Foster open communication and create a culture of inclusion
c) Discourage feedback and limit discussions
d) Rely on top-down decision-making without consulting staff

Correct answers:

1- B

2- B

3- B

4- B

5- B

11.7 Case Study: Crisis Management During the COVID-19 Pandemic at St. James Hospital

St. James Hospital was at the forefront of the COVID-19 pandemic, managing a significant influx of patients while ensuring staff safety and maintaining essential operations. Leadership quickly established emergency protocols, reallocated resources, and developed contingency plans to address the shortage of personal protective equipment (PPE). The hospital leadership also regularly communicated with staff and patients, informing them of changes and protocols. St. James Hospital successfully navigated the crisis through rapid decision-making and effective crisis management while maintaining staff morale.

Discussion Questions:

1. How did St. James Hospital's leadership respond to the resource allocation and staff safety crisis?

2. What communication strategies were used to ensure staff and patients were informed during the crisis?

3. How did effective crisis management contribute to maintaining care quality and staff morale?

4. What lessons can be learned from St. James Hospital's response to the pandemic that can be applied in future crises?

Chapter 12: Performance Management and Accountability

Healthcare organizations are constantly pressured to improve patient care, enhance operational efficiency, and maintain financial sustainability. Effective performance management is critical for achieving these objectives. This module explores strategies for setting goals, evaluating outcomes, coaching and mentoring staff, and addressing underperformance, all essential for building a high-performing healthcare organization.

12.1 Setting Goals and Evaluating Outcomes

Setting clear, measurable goals is essential for healthcare organizations to achieve their desired outcomes. Performance management starts with goal setting, which should align with the organization's overall mission and vision. By setting SMART (Specific, Measurable, Achievable, Relevant, Time-bound) goals, healthcare leaders can ensure that teams have clear objectives to work toward and that progress can be easily measured.

Using SMART Goals to Drive Performance

SMART goal setting is a well-established method for creating achievable targets. Healthcare leaders should encourage their teams to set individual and team goals aligned with the organization's strategic priorities. Leaders can track progress and identify improvement areas by ensuring that objectives are specific and measurable. Achieving these goals enhances performance, boosts morale, and ensures that the organization moves in the right direction.

12.2 Coaching and Mentorship in Healthcare

Coaching and mentorship are crucial for developing healthcare staff's skills and leadership abilities. Leaders must invest time and resources in guiding their teams and helping them reach their full potential. Coaching and mentorship not only improve individual performance but also contribute to the development of future healthcare leaders.

Developing Future Leaders Through Coaching

Effective healthcare leaders should prioritize coaching as part of their leadership strategy. Coaching involves providing personalized feedback and support to help staff improve their performance, develop new skills, and prepare for future leadership roles. By actively engaging in coaching, leaders help their teams build confidence, improve job satisfaction, and enhance patient care.

Establishing a Mentorship Culture

Mentorship is a key strategy for developing leadership talent within healthcare organizations. Leaders should create opportunities for senior staff to mentor junior staff members, fostering knowledge transfer and career growth. A strong mentorship culture encourages professional development, strengthens team cohesion, and helps to retain talented staff.

12.3 Addressing Underperformance

Addressing underperformance is a critical aspect of performance management. Leaders must be able to identify when staff are not meeting expectations and take appropriate action to address the issue. This requires balancing constructive feedback and offering support for improvement.

Providing Constructive Feedback

Providing constructive feedback involves identifying areas for improvement in a supportive and growth-focused way. Leaders must approach underperformance empathetically, offering solutions and resources to help staff overcome challenges. Feedback should be specific, actionable, and framed positively to encourage improvement.

Implementing Performance Improvement Plans

In cases where performance issues persist, leaders may need to implement formal performance improvement plans (PIPs). A PIP outlines specific expectations, timelines for improvement, and support mechanisms to help the employee succeed. Leaders must approach this process by focusing on support and development and ensuring employees understand the steps necessary to meet performance expectations.

12.4 Quick Check 

1. What is the purpose of setting SMART goals in healthcare organizations?

a) To create vague, long-term objectives
b) To provide clear, measurable targets that can be tracked
c) To ensure flexibility and avoid performance evaluation
d) To reduce accountability among staff

2. How can healthcare leaders develop future leaders within their teams?

a) By focusing solely on technical skills training
b) By providing coaching and mentorship opportunities for career growth
c) By avoiding leadership roles for junior staff members
d) By promoting staff based only on tenure

3. What should leaders do when addressing underperformance in healthcare staff?

a) Ignore the issue and let the employee resolve it independently
b) Provide constructive feedback and create performance improvement plans (PIPs)
c) Reprimand staff publicly to maintain authority
d) Allow underperforming staff to continue without intervention

4. Which of the following is an essential aspect of coaching in healthcare?

a) Providing only negative feedback
b) Offering personalized guidance and support for skill improvement
c) Focusing on team performance over individual growth
d) Ignoring employees' developmental needs

5. What is a critical element of establishing a mentorship culture in healthcare?

a) Only senior staff should participate in mentorship activities
b) Encouraging professional development and knowledge transfer between senior and junior staff
c) Limiting mentorship to administrative staff only
d) Avoiding mentorship due to time constraints

Correct answers:

1- B

2- B

3- B

4- B

5- B

12.5 Case Study: Implementing a New Electronic Health Record System at Maplewood Clinic

Maplewood Clinic implemented a new electronic health record (EHR) system to improve patient data management and streamline communication between healthcare providers. However, the transition posed significant challenges, including staff resistance, workflow disruptions, and data migration issues. Leadership conducted extensive training, provided ongoing support, and engaged staff in the change process to ensure a smooth transition. After overcoming initial hurdles, the clinic experienced improved patient care, more efficient workflows, and enhanced data security.

Discussion Questions:

1. What challenges did Maplewood Clinic face during the EHR system implementation?

2. How did the leadership team address resistance to change from staff?

3. How did the new EHR system improve patient care and operational efficiency?

4. What strategies can healthcare leaders use to manage change effectively during large-scale technology implementations?

Chapter 13: Future of Healthcare Leadership

The healthcare sector is undergoing significant transformations due to advancements in technology, changing patient needs, and the evolving demands of the workforce. Healthcare leaders must stay ahead of these changes to ensure their organizations thrive in a rapidly shifting environment. The future of healthcare leadership revolves around adopting emerging technologies, embracing sustainable practices, and fostering a culture of lifelong learning. This module explores these critical areas, providing strategies for leaders to navigate future challenges and lead their organizations toward long-term success.

13.1 Emerging Technologies and Their Impact

As technology advances exponentially, its impact on healthcare is profound and multifaceted. Technologies like artificial intelligence (AI), telemedicine, and electronic health records (EHR) are reshaping how healthcare is delivered and managed. For healthcare leaders, integrating these technologies is no longer optional but necessary to improve patient care, optimize operational efficiency, and remain competitive.

1. Artificial Intelligence in Healthcare

AI has the potential to revolutionize healthcare by enhancing diagnostic accuracy, personalizing treatment plans, and improving patient outcomes. AI algorithms are already being used to interpret medical images, predict patient outcomes, and identify patterns in clinical data that might be missed by human practitioners (Topol, 2019). Healthcare leaders must champion the adoption of AI technologies and ensure that staff members are adequately trained to use these tools effectively.

AI can also help reduce administrative burdens, improve workflow efficiency, and support decision-making. By automating routine tasks, such as processing billing or scheduling appointments, AI allows healthcare providers to focus more on patient care. However, leaders must also be aware of ethical considerations, such as data privacy and the potential for algorithmic biases, and ensure that AI systems are implemented to maintain patient trust.

2. Telemedicine and Remote Healthcare Delivery

Telemedicine is another transformative technology that is changing how healthcare is delivered. By allowing healthcare providers to consult with patients remotely, telemedicine improves access to care, particularly for patients in rural or underserved areas. It also enhances patient convenience, reducing travel and wait times, which is especially valuable in chronic disease management and post-surgical follow-ups.

For healthcare leaders, the successful integration of telemedicine requires robust infrastructure, including reliable internet access, secure video conferencing platforms, and adequate training for healthcare providers and patients. Leaders must also address regulatory challenges, such as reimbursement policies and licensure requirements, to ensure that telemedicine services are sustainable and compliant with healthcare laws.

3. Electronic Health Records (EHR) and Data Management

Electronic Health Records (EHR) are central to modern healthcare systems. EHRs streamline patient information management, improve communication among healthcare providers, and enhance the quality of patient care. However, the full potential of EHR systems can only be realized when data is used effectively to inform clinical decisions, improve patient outcomes, and enhance operational efficiency.

Healthcare leaders must ensure that their organizations' EHR systems are fully integrated with other technologies, such as AI and telemedicine platforms, to create a seamless experience for patients and healthcare providers. Additionally, leaders must advocate for data privacy and cybersecurity measures to protect sensitive patient information from breaches.

13.2 Sustainable Leadership Practices

Sustainability in healthcare leadership goes beyond environmental considerations; it involves creating organizational practices that balance economic, social, and ecological goals. Leaders must ensure that their organizations remain financially viable while promoting a culture of social responsibility and environmental stewardship. Sustainability also requires leaders to address the health needs of future populations while ensuring that resources are allocated efficiently and equitably.

1. Balancing Organizational Success with Long-Term Sustainability

Sustainable healthcare leadership focuses on long-term organizational success while addressing the challenges posed by limited resources, increasing patient demands, and rising healthcare costs. Leaders must adopt a strategic vision that prioritizes cost-efficiency, operational sustainability, and the delivery of high-quality care.

For example, investing in preventive care can reduce long-term costs by preventing chronic diseases and reducing hospital readmissions. Leaders should also focus on creating a culture of continuous improvement, where resources are allocated effectively, and operational practices are optimized for financial sustainability and enhanced patient care.

2. Environmental and Social Sustainability

Healthcare organizations also face growing pressure to become more environmentally sustainable. As healthcare systems are large consumers of energy and resources, leaders must prioritize initiatives that reduce their operations' carbon footprint. This includes energy-efficient buildings, waste reduction programs, and sustainable materials sourcing. Additionally, healthcare organizations should be mindful of their social impact, particularly regarding access to care, equity, and community involvement.

Leaders must also recognize that sustainability is linked to social equity. Healthcare organizations should work to reduce disparities in care by ensuring that all patients, regardless of socioeconomic status, have access to quality healthcare services. Leaders can implement outreach programs, community partnerships, and policy advocacy strategies to address these inequalities.

13.3 Corporate Social Responsibility (CSR) in Healthcare

Corporate Social Responsibility (CSR) in healthcare refers to the commitment of healthcare organizations to act ethically and contribute to the well-being of society. This includes addressing healthcare services' social, environmental, and economic impacts while focusing on patient care. CSR initiatives in healthcare may involve improving access to care for underserved populations, reducing the carbon footprint of healthcare operations, and implementing sustainable practices such as waste reduction and energy efficiency. Healthcare organizations also engage in social responsibility by ensuring equitable healthcare delivery, supporting community health initiatives, and prioritizing the welfare of their employees and patients. By adopting CSR principles, healthcare leaders can foster trust and credibility, enhance patient satisfaction, and promote long-term sustainability in their organizations.

13.4 Lifelong Learning as a Leader

Healthcare is an ever-evolving field, and the role of leadership is no exception. Continuous professional development is critical for healthcare leaders to stay current with emerging trends, evolving technologies, and best practices. Lifelong learning enables leaders to adapt to changes in the healthcare landscape and provides them with the skills necessary to lead organizations effectively.

1. Developing Future Leaders

To ensure the continued success of healthcare organizations, leaders must invest in developing the next generation of healthcare leaders. This includes mentoring, providing opportunities for skill development, and fostering a culture that encourages leadership at all levels. By developing future leaders, healthcare organizations can build a strong pipeline of talent equipped to handle future challenges.

Healthcare leaders must also focus on their development. Participating in leadership development programs, attending professional conferences, and engaging with peers can provide leaders with the tools and insights to navigate complex healthcare systems.

2. Fostering a Culture of Lifelong Learning

A culture of lifelong learning within an organization promotes continuous improvement and ensures that healthcare teams remain adaptable and innovative. Leaders must encourage staff to pursue ongoing education, provide access to training programs, and create environments that support knowledge-sharing and collaboration.

This culture extends to embracing modern technologies and methodologies, from clinical advancements to administrative processes. A healthcare organization that values continuous learning is better positioned to innovate, adapt to new challenges, and provide better patient care.

13.5 Quick Check

1. Which of the following is key for healthcare leaders to stay ahead in a rapidly changing healthcare environment?

a) Focusing only on patient care
b) Embracing emerging technologies and fostering lifelong learning
c) Reducing the workforce
d) Limiting access to healthcare services

2. What is one of the primary challenges of integrating artificial intelligence (AI) in healthcare?

a) AI can replace human practitioners entirely
b) Ensuring data privacy and addressing potential biases in algorithms
c) AI does not improve healthcare outcomes
d) AI systems are not cost-effective for healthcare organizations

3. How does telemedicine primarily benefit patients?

a) It reduces healthcare costs by eliminating all in-person visits
b) It improves access to care, particularly for patients in remote or underserved areas
c) It focuses on administrative tasks rather than clinical care
d) It restricts the range of services offered to patients

4. What is the role of sustainability in healthcare leadership?

a) To focus only on the financial aspects of healthcare
b) To balance economic, social, and environmental goals to ensure long-term success
c) To reduce patient care and services in Favor of cost-cutting measures
d) To prioritize short-term financial gains over long-term outcomes

5. Why is lifelong learning important for healthcare leaders?

a) To avoid technological advancements in Favor of traditional methods
b) To stay current with emerging trends and evolving technologies in healthcare
c) To limit the scope of leadership responsibilities
d) To delegate all decision-making to subordinates

Correct answers:

1- B

2- B

3- B

4- B

5- B

13.6 Case Study: Sustainability in Healthcare Leadership

Case Study: Green Hospital Initiative

A primary healthcare provider, "Healthy Future Healthcare," embarked on a sustainability initiative to reduce its operations' environmental impact. The organization implemented energy-efficient building designs, renewable energy sources, water conservation programs, and waste reduction practices. Additionally, the hospital introduced a green supply chain strategy, working with suppliers who shared the organization's commitment to sustainability. As part of this initiative, the hospital also invested in telemedicine technologies, reducing the need for patient travel and thus lowering its carbon footprint. Over three years, Healthy Future Healthcare achieved a 30% reduction in energy consumption and a 25% decrease in waste output. The sustainability program contributed to environmental goals, improved community relations, and reduced operational costs.

Discussion Questions:

1. How did Healthy Future Healthcare's sustainability initiative align with the concept of corporate social responsibility in healthcare?

2. What were the key environmental practices implemented in the Green Hospital Initiative, and how did they contribute to its sustainability goals?

3. How did the integration of telemedicine contribute to the hospital's sustainability efforts?

4. What challenges might healthcare leaders face when implementing sustainability initiatives, and how can these be overcome?

5. How does focusing on sustainability benefit the organization and the community in the long term?

Bibliography [Section 1]

• Baker, S. A., McMahon, M. M., & Hale, R. L. (2017). Communication in healthcare: An overview of strategies for improving communication in interdisciplinary teams. Journal of Healthcare Management, 62(2), 124-136.

• Benmira, S., & Agboola, M. (2021). Leadership: An evolving concept. BMJ Leader, 5(1), 3–5. https://doi.org/10.1136/leader-2020-000296

• Bennett, T. (2017). Managing underperformance in healthcare settings: A practical guide. Healthcare Management Review, 42(3), 219-226.

• Betancourt, J. R., Green, A. R., & Carrillo, E. D. (2003). Cultural competence in health care: Emerging frameworks and practical approaches—the Commonwealth Fund.

• Buntin, M. B., Burke, M. F., & Hoaglin, M. C. (2011). The benefits of health information technology: A recent literature review shows predominantly positive results. Health Affairs, 30(3), 464-471.

• Brownell, J. (2012). Listening: Attitudes, principles, and skills (6th ed.). Pearson.

• Clutterbuck, D. (2015). The mentor's guide: Facilitating effective learning relationships. Kogan Page.

• Codier, E., Freel, M., Kamikawa, C., & Morrison, P. (2009). Emotional intelligence, performance, and retention in clinical staff nurses. Nursing Administration Quarterly, 33(4), 310-316.

• Covey, S. M. R. (2006). The Speed of Trust: The One Thing that Changes Everything. Free Press.

• Day, D. V. (2001). Leadership development: A review in context. The Leadership Quarterly, 11(4), 581-613.

• Doran, G. T. (1981). There's a SMART way to write management's goals and objectives. Management Review, 70(11), 35-36.

• Gerstner, C. R., & Day, D. V. (1997). A meta-analytic review of leader behavior: A test of the leader categorization theory of leadership. Journal of Applied Psychology, 82(5), 755-768.

- Glickman, C. D., & Gordon, D. (2018). The complete guide to coaching in healthcare. McGraw-Hill.

- Glickman, S. W., Baggett, K. A., Krubert, C. G., Peterson, E. D., & Schulman, K. A. (2007). Promoting quality: the health-care organization from a management perspective. International Journal for Quality in Health Care, 19(6), 341-348.

- Goleman, D. (2000). Leadership that gets results. Harvard Business Review, 78(2), 78-90.

- Goodwin, N. (2016). The challenge of managing a patient-centred health system: Lessons from the UK NHS. Journal of Health Organization and Management, 30(3), 423-437.

- Hrebiniak, L. G. (2005). Making strategy work: Leading effective execution and change. Wharton School Publishing.

- Hersey, P., & Blanchard, K. H. (1969). Management of organizational behavior: Utilizing human resources. Prentice-Hall.

- Kaplan, R. S., & Norton, D. P. (2001). The strategy-focused organization: How balanced scorecard companies thrive in the new business environment. Harvard Business Press.

- Kahn, J. M., & Daugherty, L. (2020). Telemedicine in the time of COVID-19: A global perspective on future trends. American Journal of Public Health, 110(4), 446-448.

- Kiwanuka, F., Nanyonga, R. C., Sak☐Dankosky, N., Muwanguzi, P. A., & Kvist, T. (2021). Nursing leadership styles and their impact on intensive care unit quality measures: An integrative review. Journal of Nursing Management, 29(2), 133-142.

- Kohn, L. T., Corrigan, J. M., & Donaldson, M. S. (2000). To err is human: Building a safer health system. National Academy Press.

- McAlearney, A. S., Robbins, J., Kowalczyk, N., Chisolm, D. J., & Song, P. H. (2013). Implementing high-performance work practices in healthcare organizations: qualitative and conceptual evidence. Journal of Healthcare Management, 58(6), 446-462.

- McKinsey & Company. (2020). Sustainability in healthcare: The next frontier. McKinsey & Company.

- Nauman, S., Bhatti, S. H., Imam, H., & Khan, M. S. (2022). How servant leadership drives project team performance through collaborative culture and knowledge sharing. Project Management Journal, 53(1), 17-32.

- Northeastern University. (2024). Healthcare management vs leadership: What's the difference? Retrieved from https://bouve.northeastern.edu/news/healthcare-management-vs-leadership-whats-the-difference/

- O'Daniel, M., & Rosenstein, A. H. (2008). Professional communication and team collaboration. In Patient safety and quality: An evidence-based handbook for nurses (pp. 271-284). Agency for Healthcare Research and Quality.

- Olatoye, F. O., Elufioye, O. A., Okoye, C. C., Nwankwo, E. E., & Oladapo, J. O. (2024). Leadership styles and their impact on healthcare management effectiveness: A review. International Journal of Science and Research Archive, 11(01), 2022–2032. https://doi.org/10.30574/ijsra.2024.11.1.0271

- Patterson, K. (2003). Servant leadership: A theoretical model. The Journal of Management Development, 22(5), 407-425.

- Quek, S. J., Thomson, L., Houghton, R., Bramley, L., Davis, S., & Cooper, J. (2021). Distributed leadership as a predictor of employee engagement, job satisfaction and turnover intention in UK nursing staff. Journal of Nursing Management, 29(6), 1544-1553.

- Raghupathi, W., & Raghupathi, V. (2014). Big data analytics in healthcare: promise and potential. Health Information Science and Systems, 2(1), 1-10.

- Sackett, D. L., Straus, S. E., Richardson, W. S., Rosenberg, W. & Haynes, R. B. (2000). Evidence-based medicine: How to practice and teach EBM. Churchill Livingstone.

- Schoemaker, P. J. H., Krupp, S., & Howland, S. (2013). Strategic leadership: The essential skills. Sloan Management Review, 54(4), 51-58.

- Schroeder, R. A., Mannion, R., & Davies, H. T. (2018). Collaborative healthcare leadership: Fostering teamwork and trust. Sage Publications.

- Senge, P. M. (2006). The fifth discipline: The art and practice of the learning organization. Doubleday.

- Stevens, E. L., Hulme, A., & Salmon, P. M. (2021). The impact of power on health care team performance and patient safety: A literature review. Ergonomics, 64(5), 657-671. https://doi.org/10.1080/00140139.2021.1906454

- Stone, D., Patton, B., & Heen, S. (2010). Difficult Conversations: How to Discuss What Matters Most. Penguin Books.

- Tannenbaum, S. I., Salas, E., & Cohen, D. (2012). Team training and teamwork in healthcare. Journal of Healthcare Management, 57(6), 435-448.

- Topol, E. (2019). Deep medicine: How artificial intelligence can make healthcare human again. Basic Books.

- Van de Bovenkamp, H., Trappenburg, M., & Grit, K. (2020). The effects of diversity on communication and teamwork in healthcare teams: A systematic review. Journal of Health Communication, 25(6), 520-530.

- Van Dierendonck, D. (2011). Servant leadership: A review and synthesis. Journal of Management, 37(4), 1228-1261.

- Wagner, E. H., & Austin, B. T. (2001). Improving outcomes for patients with chronic illness. The role of collaborative management. Health Affairs, 20(1), 64-78.

- West, M. A., & Richter, A. (2008). The challenge of leadership in healthcare. BMJ, 336(7639), 305-307.

- Wheeler, S., & Thielemans, K. (2019). Healthcare leadership: A practical guide. Routledge.

- Williams, S. (2020). The role of digital technology in transforming healthcare. Digital Health, 6, 205520762092106.

- Austin, E. J., Evans, P., Goldwater, R., & Potter, V. (2007). A preliminary study of first-year medical students' emotional intelligence, empathy, and exam performance. Personality and Individual Differences, 39(8), 1395–1405.

- Beckham, D. (1995). Physician leadership: Redefining the future. Physician Executive Journal, 21(11), 14–21.

- Cherry, M. (2021). Emotional intelligence and leadership effectiveness in hospitalist medical directors. Organization Development Journal, 39(1), 30–35.

- Deshpande, S. P., & Joseph, J. (2009). Impact of emotional intelligence, ethical behavior, and leadership effectiveness in healthcare administration. Journal of Business Ethics, 90(3), 447–464.

- Gay, L. R., Mills, G. E., & Airasian, P. (2006). Educational research: Competencies for analysis and applications (8th ed.). Pearson.

- Gerbarg, Z. (2002). Leadership and organizational development in healthcare. Journal of Healthcare Management, 47(2), 85–93.

- McMullen, P. (2002). Understanding physician training and biases in emotional intelligence. Medical Education Quarterly, 5(2), 112–119.

Section Two:

Leading Change in Healthcare

Chapter 14: Why Change is Important in Healthcare

Learning objectives

- Recall key terms and concepts related to change in healthcare.

- Explain why change is necessary in healthcare settings.

- Understand and describe the impact of change on healthcare outcomes.

14.1 Introduction to Change in Healthcare

Change in healthcare is not just a trend; it's a necessity. The industry, like many others, is constantly evolving. The volume and quality of demand are constantly in flux, and the external environment for healthcare organizations is ever-changing. In this dynamic landscape, the ability to adapt and innovate is not just beneficial; it's crucial for survival.

Significant advances in our understanding of diseases and the context of healthcare service delivery make change a logical response. By adapting to these new expectations, organizations cannot only survive but thrive in the current context. Change is not just about keeping up; it's about improving and enhancing the services we provide.

Also, apart from the advancement in understanding the disease process and different new models of treatment, the patients, their families, and the community's understanding of the nature of what health means and the consequent change in expectations lead to newly broader objectives of what healthcare organizations should provide to their customers.

Healthcare organizations' external environment, including the different market components, regulations, scientific research, and technology advancement, among other factors, sets the pace they should adopt. Otherwise, they might risk being kicked off the market soon.

• Definition and Key Concepts Related to Change in Healthcare Settings

Change in healthcare refers to the processes, adaptations, and transformations that occur within healthcare systems, practices, and policies to improve service delivery and patient outcomes. Key concepts include:

• Organizational Change: Refers to the planned transformation of a healthcare organization's structure, culture, or processes to enhance performance and meet evolving demands.

• Quality Improvement: The systematic efforts to improve healthcare services, enhancing patient care quality and safety through data-driven strategies.

• Change Management: The structured approach to transitioning individuals, teams, and organizations from a current state to a desired future state, ensuring that change is implemented smoothly and sustainably.

• Stakeholder Engagement: Involvement of all parties affected by changes, including patients, healthcare providers, administrators, and policymakers, ensuring their insights and feedback guide the change process.

Overview of the Evolving Nature of Healthcare: Trends, Challenges, and Advancements

The healthcare landscape is constantly evolving due to various trends, challenges, and advancements:

o   **Trends:**

• Patient-centered Care: There is an increasing emphasis on tailoring healthcare services to individual patient needs, preferences, and values. Amid all the challenges that healthcare demands face from the public health perspective, customized patient-centered care remains a priority. People, and therefore patients, differ in their priorities and expectations. This is a significant concept to consider when planning healthcare delivery.

• Telehealth Expansion: Rapid growth in telemedicine services, driven by technological advancements and a shift towards remote care options.

• Value-Based Care: Transition from fee-for-service models to value-based care, focusing on patient outcomes and cost-efficiency.

o   **Challenges:**

• Regulatory Changes: Ongoing changes in healthcare policies and regulations require organizations to adapt their practices to remain compliant.

• Healthcare Disparities: Persistent inequalities in access to and quality of care necessitating targeted interventions and reforms.

• Aging Population: The aging population challenges healthcare by increasing demand for services and chronic conditions, straining resources, and raising costs. It may also lead to shortages of geriatric professionals and fragmented care, necessitating effective management strategies.

• Workforce Shortages: Challenges in recruiting and retaining skilled healthcare professionals, impacting service delivery and patient care.

o	**Advancements:**

• Health Information Technology (HIT): Increased adoption of electronic health records (EHRs), data analytics, and health information exchanges to enhance communication and decision-making.

• Personalized Medicine: Growing use of genomics and biotechnology to tailor treatments to individual patient profiles, improving effectiveness.

• Artificial Intelligence (AI): Integrating AI and machine learning to support diagnostic processes, optimize operations, and predict patient outcomes.

14.2 The Necessity for Change

As discussed before, change in healthcare has become necessary for many reasons. Let's explore some in more detail.

Improving Patient Outcomes: Change is essential to enhance the quality and safety of patient care. By implementing evidence-based practices, organizations can reduce medical errors, improve recovery times, and enhance patient satisfaction. Continuous evaluation and adaptation of clinical practices ensure that patients receive the best possible care.

Enhancing Healthcare Systems: Change makes healthcare systems more efficient and effective. Streamlining processes, reducing waste, and improving resource allocation led to better service delivery. Additionally, integrating multidisciplinary teams and fostering collaboration among healthcare providers can enhance care coordination, benefiting patient health.

Keeping Up with Technology and Regulations: The rapid pace of technological advancements necessitates that healthcare organizations continuously adapt to stay relevant. Embracing new tools like telemedicine platforms and health data analytics is crucial for improving efficiency and patient engagement. Moreover, regulation changes require organizations to remain compliant, ensuring they meet legal and ethical standards while providing safe and effective care.

The previous reasons could be examples of what makes it crucial for healthcare organizations to change. However, this is not an exhaustive list, as the list goes on and might change from one organization to another. Again, as the external environment around the organizations changes, they must change, too. The idea is simple: Organisations cannot stand still while the world changes, expecting they might survive. This is far from a logical possibility.

14.3 Case Study

Case Overview

Valley Community Health Centre is a small, rural healthcare facility serving a diverse population, including many patients with limited access to transportation. The management team has decided to implement telehealth services to improve patient access to care. While some staff members are excited about the modern technology, others are skeptical about its effectiveness and the changes it will bring to their workflow.

Context

Current Situation:

• High no-show rates for in-person appointments due to transportation issues.

• A growing number of patients with chronic conditions require regular follow-up.

• Recent advancements in telehealth technology make remote consultations feasible.

Change Initiative Goals:

o Increase patient access to healthcare services by 30% through telehealth.

o Reduce no-show rates by 25% within six months.

o Ensure that at least 70% of healthcare providers feel confident using the new telehealth system within three months of implementation.

Discussion Questions:

Identifying Challenges:

o What challenges do you anticipate in implementing telehealth services in this community health center?

o How might patient demographics (e.g., age, technological literacy) impact the adoption of telehealth?

Staff Concerns:

o What specific concerns might staff have regarding the transition to telehealth services?

o How can these concerns be addressed to ensure buy-in from all team members?

Training and Support:

o What training and resources do healthcare providers need to use telehealth technology effectively?

o How can the management ensure ongoing support and troubleshooting for staff as they adapt to the new system?

Patient Engagement:

o What strategies can be implemented to educate patients about the benefits of telehealth?

o How can the healthcare team ensure patients feel comfortable and confident using telehealth services?

Measuring Success:

o What metrics should be used to evaluate the effectiveness of the telehealth program?

o How can the team gather feedback from patients and providers to continuously improve the telehealth experience?

Ethical Considerations:

o What ethical considerations should be considered when implementing telehealth services?

o How can the organization ensure that the transition to remote care does not disadvantage vulnerable populations?

Chapter 15: Drivers of Change in Healthcare

Learning objectives

- Understand and identify key drivers of change in healthcare.

- Apply knowledge to recognize how different drivers affect healthcare organizations.

The need for change mostly comes from outside the organization based on the changing external environment. However, this is not exclusive, as internal factors might trigger change. Higher management's intention to change the organization's mission, vision, or significant goal entails change that varies in scope depending on the number, size, and criticality of the functions affected inside the organization.

This section will discuss the key drivers of change in healthcare and how they impact healthcare organizations. We will explore familiar internal and external drivers of change in the healthcare setting.

15.1 Internal Drivers of Change

a. Workforce dynamics and social expectations:

Healthcare organizations need to adapt their workforce to meet the changing needs of patients and the healthcare industry. This includes addressing issues such as staffing shortages and ensuring that the right skills and expertise are available. The shortage of healthcare professionals is a significant issue that affects many healthcare organizations worldwide. The first natural response to that is usually trying to attract qualified professionals from around the globe. However, this is not typically easy or accessible to some organizations, which, in turn, necessitates some internal change to ameliorate the impact of this shortage. This might come in change projects that aim at improving the skills of the current staff, using technology to save professionals 'time for more precious tasks and the like. Successful organizations always keep in mind that people make a difference. Therefore, the leadership should take care of employees as internal customers of the organization. This involves their changing needs that should be considered for validation, and then they should try to secure them as implied by the organizational resources. External environment changes affect both the organization from one side and the employees as individuals. This might be a valid reason for making organizational changes to support the employees who will support their organizations.

b. Cost management and financial pressures:

Healthcare organizations must manage costs efficiently while providing high-quality care. They must find ways to reduce expenses without compromising patient outcomes.

c. Shareholders' expectations:

 Healthcare organizations must consider the expectations of their shareholders, such as investors and board members. They need to focus on financial performance and ensure a return on investment.

d. Internal resources and capabilities:

Healthcare organizations need to assess their internal resources and capacities to identify areas for improvement and develop change strategies.

15.2 External Drivers of Change

a. Digitalization:

- Digitalizing healthcare processes and systems has significantly impacted how healthcare is delivered. It includes using digital tools, such as electronic prescribing and appointment scheduling systems, to streamline and enhance care delivery.

- EHR (Electronic Health Records): The adoption and integration of electronic health records have transformed healthcare delivery. EHRs allow for efficient storage, retrieval, and sharing of patient information, resulting in improved patient care coordination.

Telemedicine: Telemedicine refers to using technology to provide remote healthcare services. It allows patients to receive care without physically visiting healthcare facilities. Telemedicine has gained popularity, especially during the COVID-19 pandemic, and has become an essential tool for healthcare organizations.

b. Regulatory and policy changes:

Compliance: Healthcare organizations must comply with various regulatory requirements to ensure patient safety, privacy, and quality of care. They must stay updated with changing regulations and make necessary changes to remain compliant.

- Accreditation: Accreditation plays a vital role in ensuring the quality and safety of healthcare organizations. Healthcare organizations strive to maintain accreditation status to demonstrate their commitment to excellence.

c. Competition:

Healthcare organizations face competition from other providers in the industry. This competition drives them to continuously improve and differentiate their services to attract patients and remain competitive.

d. Savvy patients: Patient expectations:

- Patients are becoming more informed and involved in their healthcare decisions. They have lofty expectations for quality care, transparency, and accessibility. Healthcare organizations need to adapt to meet these evolving patient expectations.

e. Globalization:

- Globalization has increased the interconnectedness of healthcare systems worldwide. Healthcare organizations must adapt to global standards and advancements to provide quality care and remain competitive internationally.

f. Demographics

- Demographics drive change in healthcare by influencing service demand and shaping health policies. Factors like age and socioeconomic status increase the need for specific services, such as chronic disease management, prompting healthcare organizations to adapt to diverse community needs.

In summary, understanding the drivers of change in healthcare is crucial for organizations to adapt to evolving needs and remain competitive. Internal and external drivers significantly shape the healthcare landscape and require careful consideration and strategic planning.

15.3 Case discussion

Overview

Med Plus Healthcare: Navigating Internal Challenges and External Pressures for Strategic Transformation

Med Plus Healthcare, a mid-sized hospital in a rapidly growing urban area, faces critical internal and external challenges that demand immediate strategic change. The hospital is dealing with a nursing shortage that impacts patient care quality and leads to staff burnout while also needing to address employee expectations for support, career growth, and work-life balance. Rising operational costs are straining finances, and the leadership team is pressured to find cost-saving measures without compromising patient outcomes. Investors expect Medplus to maintain profitability amidst evolving demands for technology and staffing improvements, yet the hospital's limited resources and outdated systems hinder its adaptability. Externally, Medplus lags behind competitors in digital healthcare offerings, such as fully integrated Electronic Health Records (EHR) and telemedicine, which patients increasingly expect. New regulations impose stricter data privacy and compliance standards, with severe penalties for non-compliance, necessitating system updates to stay compliant. Nearby hospitals with advanced digital services draw patients who value convenience and accessibility. At the same time, Medplus must also cater to a growing, diverse, and aging population with specific healthcare needs like chronic disease management.

Discussion prompts

- What initiatives can Medplus implement to address the nursing shortage while improving staff retention and morale?

- How can Medplus manage rising costs effectively, ensuring patient outcomes are not compromised?

- What strategies should Medplus adopt to meet shareholder expectations while balancing financial performance and patient care?

Chapter 16: Inhibitors of Change in Healthcare

Learning objectives

• Understand common inhibitors to change in healthcare organizations.

• Analyse case studies to determine how barriers contributed to failures.

• Evaluate different strategies to overcome resistance and other inhibitors.

16.1 Internal Barriers to Change

Lack of Leadership Commitment

Effective change initiatives require strong leadership support. When leaders are not fully committed, it can lead to a lack of direction, inadequate resources, and insufficient motivation among staff. Leaders must actively engage with their teams, articulate the vision for change, and model the behaviors they wish to see in their organizations. Resistance** Resistance to change is a common phenomenon in healthcare settings. Staff may feel threatened by the unknown or be comfortable with existing practices. This resistance can hinder the implementation of new initiatives. Understanding the root causes of resistance, such as fear of job loss or increased workload, is critical for addressing these issues.

Cultural inertia

Healthcare organizations often have deeply embedded cultures that can be resistant to change. Cultural inertia can manifest in practices, beliefs, and norms prioritizing tradition over innovation. Fulfilling a culture that values flexibility and continuous improvement is essential to counteract this inertia.

Financial limitations

Financial constraints can significantly impede change initiatives. Budget limitations may restrict investment in modern technologies, training programs, or necessary infrastructure. Organizations must prioritize strategic spending and seek funding opportunities to facilitate change.

Resource Limitations

Limited human and physical resources can be a barrier to change. Insufficient staff or inadequate technological infrastructure can prevent organizations from successfully implementing new initiatives. Assessing resource availability and reallocating existing resources may help mitigate these limitations.

Workforce Limitations

Unskilled healthcare professionals can create challenges in implementing change. If the workforce lacks the necessary skills or knowledge, it can lead to ineffective change processes. Ongoing training and development programs are essential for equipping staff to embrace and enact change.

Fear of Failure

Fear of failure discourages staff from embracing change. This fear may stem from previous unsuccessful initiatives or a lack of confidence in new processes. Creating a supportive environment that encourages experimentation and learning from mistakes is crucial for overcoming this barrier.

Resistance to New Technology

As healthcare evolves, the technology is used to deliver care. However, some staff members may resist adopting modern technologies due to discomfort with change or skepticism about their effectiveness. Providing comprehensive training and demonstrating the benefits of new technologies can help alleviate these concerns.

16.2 External Barriers to Change

- Customer Preferences
- Competition
- Supplier Dynamics
- Economic Conditions
- Regulatory Environment
- Technological Advancements

Customer Preferences

Patients increasingly seek personalized care, convenience, and quality. Their preferences influence service offerings like telehealth options and patient-centered care models.

Competition

Healthcare providers, including hospitals, clinics, and telehealth services, compete for patients based on quality, cost, and accessibility. Competitive pressures can drive innovation and improve service delivery.

Supplier Dynamics

The availability and pricing of medical supplies, pharmaceuticals, and technology affect healthcare providers' operational costs and the quality of care. Supplier relationships are critical for ensuring timely access to necessary resources.

Economic Conditions

Economic factors, such as employment rates and insurance coverage, influence patients' ability to access healthcare services. Economic downturns can lead to reduced healthcare spending by both consumers and providers.

Regulatory Environment

Healthcare is heavily regulated, with laws affecting everything from patient privacy (e.g., HIPAA) to billing practices and quality standards. Regulatory changes can impact operational procedures and compliance requirements for healthcare organizations.

Technological Advancements

Innovations in medical technology, electronic health records, and telemedicine are transforming healthcare delivery. Modern technologies can enhance patient care, improve efficiency, and drive competitive advantage.

16.3 Strategies to Overcome Barriers

- Leadership Buy-In: from leaders is crucial. Leaders should communicate the vision for change and involve staff in planning to foster ownership and accountability.

- Staff Engagement: Actively involving staff in decision-making can reduce resistance. Regular feedback sessions and open communication channels trust and increase engagement.

Patient-Centric Approach

Adopting a patient-centric approach can drive meaningful change. Organizations should prioritize patient needs and preferences more than ever. By actively engaging patients and gathering feedback, healthcare providers can tailor their services to enhance patient satisfaction and outcomes.

Transforming the Patient Experience

Improving the overall patient experience can also facilitate change. Organizations should streamline processes, adapt, and utilize technology to provide a seamless and positive patient experience. This transformation can lead to greater patient loyalty and improved health outcomes.

16.4 Case discussion

Overcoming Internal Barriers at Valley Health Clinic: Leadership, Culture, and Resource Challenges in Healthcare Transformation.

Scenario:

Valley Health Clinic is a regional healthcare provider striving to improve patient care and efficiency by adopting modern technology and updated patient care protocols. However, internal barriers are stalling these change initiatives. While supportive, the leadership team has not provided clear, consistent communication or dedicated resources, causing staff confusion and a lack of motivation. The clinic's profoundly ingrained culture prioritizes traditional practices, with many employees resistant to adopting new methods. Limited budgets restrict investment in essential technology and training, and the clinic is operating with a tight workforce, where some staff members lack the necessary skills for modernized healthcare delivery. Staff are also wary of the changes, with an intense fear of failure due to past unsuccessful initiatives. These internal issues collectively inhibit the clinic's efforts to improve patient care and meet rising healthcare standards.

Discussion prompts

o How can Valley Health Clinic's leadership team demonstrate a more substantial commitment to this change initiative?

o What specific actions should leaders take to provide clear communication and resources for this project?

o What steps can be taken to address the clinic's cultural resistance to new practices and encourage a more flexible, improvement-focused environment?

o How can the clinic reduce employees' fear of failure and foster a culture that supports experimentation and learning?

16.5 Case discussion

Navigating External Pressures at MetroMed Health Services: Adapting to Competition, Economic Shifts, and Regulatory Demands

MetroMed Health Services is a large healthcare provider in a competitive metropolitan area. MetroMed plans to expand telehealth services and improve digital patient records to stay competitive, but several external factors present challenges. Patients increasingly prefer personalized, accessible care, demanding in-person and remote healthcare options. Competing hospitals in the area already offer advanced digital services, placing pressure on MetroMed to keep up. Additionally, recent economic downturns have affected patients' ability to afford healthcare, impacting MetroMed's revenue. On top of this, regulatory changes related to patient data protection require costly upgrades to digital systems for compliance.

Limited access to certain critical medical supplies due to supply chain disruptions further affects MetroMed's operational efficiency. The leadership team is unsure how to navigate these external pressures while meeting patient expectations and maintaining a competitive edge.

Discussion prompts

o How can MetroMed adapt its services to meet evolving expectations for personalized, accessible care?

o What strategies could MetroMed employ to differentiate itself from competing hospitals offering advanced digital services?

o How should MetroMed address challenges with supplier access to ensure a steady supply of critical medical materials?

o Considering recent economic downturns, what actions can MetroMed take to support patients who may be financially impacted while sustaining its revenue?

Chapter 17: How Change Happens: Models of Leading Change

Learning objectives

- Apply different change management models to real-life healthcare scenarios.

- Analyse the strengths and weaknesses of each model when leading change in healthcare organizations.

Change in healthcare organizations

17.1 Change Management Models

Lewin's Change Management Model

Kurt Lewin's Change Management Model consists of three stages: Unfreeze, Change, and Refreeze.

Unfreeze: This initial stage involves preparing for change by recognizing the need for change and creating motivation. In healthcare, this might include assessing current practices, identifying areas for improvement, and communicating the reasons for the change to all stakeholders.

Change: This is the actual transition phase. New processes, systems, or behaviors are implemented. This could involve introducing modern technology, altering workflows, or changing team structures in a healthcare setting. Continuous support and communication are vital to help staff adapt during this stage.

Refreeze: Once changes are made, the organization must stabilize and solidify them as the new norm. This involves reinforcing the new practices through policies, training, and recognition to integrate them into the organizational culture (Burnes, 2004).

Kotter's 8-Step Model

In healthcare, Kotter's 8-Step Change Model is particularly relevant, as it provides a structured framework for navigating complex changes in medical settings. According to a recent article by Burch and Roberts (2020), these steps are instrumental in ensuring that change initiatives not only take root but also lead to improved patient outcomes and operational efficiency in medical environments:

• Create a Sense of Urgency: Communicate the need for change to inspire stakeholders. This initial step is crucial in generating enthusiasm and readiness for change, highlighting the risks of inaction and the potential benefits of moving forward. A keen sense of urgency can motivate team members to commit to the change initiative.

• Build a Guiding Coalition: Assemble a group of influential leaders and stakeholders to support the change effort. This coalition should include diverse perspectives and expertise, fostering a strong, unified front to champion the change. Their leadership is essential for guiding the organization through the complexities of the change process.

• From a Strategic Vision: Develop an unobstructed vision that guides the change initiative and helps others understand its importance. A well-articulated vision provides direction and sets expectations, ensuring all stakeholders align with the change's goals.

• Enlist a Volunteer Army: Share the vision widely and regularly to keep everyone informed and engaged. This step focuses on fostering broad support for the change by communicating the vision in an accessible way, encouraging individuals at all levels to take ownership of the initiative.

• Enable Action by Removing Barriers: Remove obstacles that hinder change, enabling staff to act toward the vision. Identifying and addressing systemic, cultural, or procedural barriers empowers individuals to pursue change without unnecessary hindrances.

- Generate Short-Term Wins: Identify and celebrate short-term successes to build momentum and support for the change. Recognizing early achievements creates a sense of accomplishment and demonstrates that the shift yields positive results, which can enhance buy-in and enthusiasm.

- Sustain Acceleration: Use early successes to drive additional change efforts and prevent regression to old behaviors. This step is about maintaining the momentum gained from initial wins and ensuring that the organization continues progressing toward its goals without falling back into previous patterns.

- Institute Change: Ensure the new practices are embedded in the organization's culture through policies, practices, and leadership support. Institutionalizing change involves reinforcing new behaviors and practices to become part of the organization's identity, ensuring long-term sustainability.

17.2 Applying Change Models in Healthcare

Change management models can be applied in clinical and administrative settings to enhance efficiency and improve patient outcomes.

Practical Applications in Clinical Settings: Implementing a new electronic health record (EHR) system may follow Lewin's model by unfreezing the current processes, training staff on the new system, and refreezing by establishing new protocols for EHR use. Kotter's model could guide this process by creating urgency for better patient data management and forming a coalition of tech-savvy staff to champion the change.

Practical Applications in Administrative Settings: A hospital might utilize Kotter's model to improve scheduling efficiency in administrative functions. By creating urgency through data on missed appointments, forming a coalition of department heads, and communicating a vision for a new scheduling system, the organization can empower staff to adopt new practices. Quick wins, such as improved appointment booking times, can be highlighted to maintain momentum.

Importance of Staff Training

Training staff is crucial in applying change management models in healthcare. Proper training ensures all team members have the necessary skills and knowledge to implement new processes effectively. This includes training on innovative technologies, workflows, and protocols introduced during the change process. By investing in staff training, healthcare organizations can enhance the likelihood of successful change implementation, improve staff confidence, and lead to better patient outcomes.

17.3 Case Discussion 1

Applying Kotter's 8-Step Model for Change in a Hospital's Patient Scheduling System

Riverside Hospital is grappling with a high rate of missed appointments and scheduling inefficiencies, resulting in long wait times, patient dissatisfaction, and decreased revenue. The hospital's leadership has implemented a new scheduling software system to streamline appointment bookings and minimize errors. To ensure the success of this initiative, they apply Kotter's 8-Step Model. The CEO begins by creating urgency by presenting data highlighting lost revenue and patient dissatisfaction from scheduling issues, effectively communicating the need for an improved system across departments, and emphasizing its potential benefits for patient care and hospital operations. Next, a powerful coalition comprises department heads, IT specialists, and enthusiastic staff members who will advocate for the change and support their teams. This coalition collaborates to create a vision of a "smoother, patient-friendly, and efficient scheduling system" to reduce wait times and enhance patient satisfaction. The vision is then

communicated widely through staff meetings, emails, and posters placed in common areas, ensuring everyone understands the importance of the new system. To empower action, staff undergo training on the latest software while addressing administrative

obstacles such as outdated policies. Following the initial rollout, the hospital celebrates early successes, including a 15% reduction in missed appointments and positive patient feedback, to build momentum. They continue to build on this change by adding

functionalities like automated appointment reminders, demonstrating the system's adaptability and commitment to ongoing improvements. Finally, the hospital updates its policies to reflect the new system. It holds staff feedback sessions to maintain engagement, with leaders regularly emphasizing the new system's value in meetings to anchor it within the hospital's culture.

Discussion prompts

1. Why is creating urgency critical in this scenario, and how does it influence staff engagement?

2. How does forming a coalition support the implementation of the scheduling system?

3. What role do quick wins play in sustaining momentum, and how can the hospital ensure these successes are celebrated?

4. Why is it necessary to anchor the scheduling system changes in the hospital's culture, and how might this be achieved?

17.4 Case Discussion 2

Applying Lewin's 3-Step Model for Introducing Telemedicine in a Community Clinic

Hillside Community Clinic, a small healthcare provider, is launching a telemedicine service to serve patients living in remote areas or those facing transportation challenges. This initiative aims to improve access to healthcare while reducing in-clinic wait times. To facilitate this change, the clinic follows Lewin's 3-Step Model. In the unfreeze stage, the clinic's leadership articulates the limitations of in-person appointments, highlighting the necessity for telemedicine to enhance patient care. They invite staff to voice their concerns and questions regarding the new system and host workshops to help everyone understand telemedicine and its potential benefits. During the change phase, the clinic begins rolling out the telemedicine service by introducing the software and providing comprehensive training for the staff. Initially, they offer telemedicine appointments to a limited number of patients, ensuring continuous support from IT and clinical leads while providing clear guidelines for handling technical issues and managing patient interactions via telemedicine. Finally, in the refreeze stage, telemedicine is formalized as a regular service option, with new policies established and ongoing training scheduled to reinforce telemedicine skills. Staff meetings routinely include discussions about telemedicine performance, ensuring this service becomes a standard part of the clinic's operations.

Discussion prompts

1. How does the "Unfreeze" step in Lewin's model, which involves preparing individuals for change by helping them understand the need for change and its benefits, help prepare the clinic staff for telemedicine?

2. What is the importance of support and training during the "Change" phase, and how does it impact the success of telemedicine?

3. How does the "Refreeze" phase ensure that telemedicine becomes a stable, integrated service at the clinic?

4. Why might Lewin's model be beneficial in a small clinic setting for implementing telemedicine?

Chapter 18: The Change Curve: How We React to Change

Learning objectives

- Understand the emotional responses to change and how they manifest in teams.

- Analyse how individuals and groups react to change and develop strategies to manage these reactions.

18.1 The Psychological Journey of Change

Understanding the Emotional Reactions: Denial, Resistance, Exploration, Acceptance

Change often triggers emotional reactions as individuals adapt to new circumstances. The four key stages include:

Denial: Initial resistance to change often stems from a reluctance to believe that change is necessary, especially in healthcare, where routines are deeply ingrained.

Resistance: As the reality of change sets in, people may resist, feeling anxious or threatened. In healthcare, resistance might stem from concerns over patient safety, workload, or the disruption of trusted processes.

Exploration: Gradually, individuals begin to explore the new situation, considering its potential benefits. This phase allows healthcare staff to learn, ask questions, and build understanding around the change.

Acceptance: In the final stage, individuals embrace the change, integrating it into their routines and seeing it as beneficial or manageable. Acceptance is key to achieving sustained progress and improved outcomes in healthcare.

The Role of Communication and Empathy in Guiding Teams through the Change Process

Effective communication and empathy are essential for supporting teams through these emotional stages. Clear, consistent communication helps dispel fears, builds trust, and ensures everyone understands the reasons behind the change. Empathy allows leaders to acknowledge team members' concerns, validate their feelings, and offer support, fostering a safe environment for adaptation. This compassionate approach is critical in healthcare, where change can directly impact patient care and staff wellbeing.

18.2 Managing Reactions to Change

Strategies for Supporting Staff and Patients through the Change Curve

Supporting staff and patients through the change curve involves targeted strategies to manage emotions and increase comfort with new processes. Key strategies include:

Providing Information and Education: Educating staff and patients about upcoming changes and their benefits can alleviate uncertainty. Clear explanations of why the change is necessary and how it will improve workflows or patient outcomes can reduce anxiety.

Encouraging Feedback and Participation: Inviting feedback gives individuals a sense of involvement, reducing resistance. Open forums, surveys, or focus groups allow staff and patients to voice concerns and feel heard, creating a collaborative environment.

Establishing Peer Support: Creating support groups or mentorship programs helps staff share experiences, ask questions, and support each other through change. For patients, peer support groups can provide comfort and understanding, significantly when change impacts their care directly.

Regular Check-Ins and Reassurance: Regularly updating and addressing ongoing concerns builds trust and keeps everyone informed. Simple check-ins with staff and patients can reinforce that their experiences and reactions are valued, creating a supportive atmosphere.

Tools to Build Resilience and Adaptability within Healthcare Teams

Building resilience and adaptability helps healthcare teams handle change more effectively. Some helpful tools include:

Training Programs: Offer training on new processes, systems, or technologies to ensure staff feel competent and confident. Training can also include soft skills, such as stress management and adaptability, which support resilience.

Mental Health and Wellness Resources: Change can be stressful, so providing access to mental health support, such as counseling, mindfulness workshops, or resilience training, helps healthcare workers manage stress and adapt better.

Change Champions: Identifying and empowering change champions within teams can foster a positive attitude towards change. These individuals act as role models, guiding others and promoting adaptability.

Flexible Adaptation Plans: Recognize that each team member may react to change differently. Tailoring support and pacing to individual needs allows teams to adapt with less resistance and more sustained commitment.

18.3 Case Discussion 1

Navigating Change: Implementing an EHR System at Greenfield Clinic.

Scenario

At Green Valley Medical Centre, leadership has announced the implementation of a new electronic health record (EHR) system to streamline patient documentation and improve data access. However, the staff's initial response is mixed, reflecting the emotional reactions that typically accompany change. In the first phase, denial, some team members express disbelief that the current system is inadequate, insisting that it works well enough and showing reluctance to accept that change is necessary. As reality sets in and training sessions begin, the staff enters the resistance phase; they voice concerns about increased workloads and potential errors during the transition, with some expressing fear over their ability to adapt to modern technology. In the exploration stage, a few enthusiastic staff members engage with the new system, seeking answers and testing its functionalities, while most remain hesitant. The management recognizes the importance of effective communication and empathy in this process and schedules regular check-ins to address ongoing concerns. As training progresses, more staff members start to embrace the EHR system. This leads to a gradual shift toward the acceptance stage, where they integrate the new system into their daily routines and recognize its benefits for patient care and workflow efficiency.

Discussion prompts

• How did the staff's emotional reactions (denial, resistance, exploration, acceptance) manifest during the implementation of the new EHR system? Provide specific examples from the scenario.

• < UNK> How did the manager's communication style influence the staff's feelings about the change? How could communication be improved to better support the team during transitions?

• How important is IT specialists and peer support's role in helping staff navigate the change curve? What specific strategies can be employed to enhance this support?

• What did the nurse raise the primary concerns regarding the new EHR system? How can management address these concerns to reduce resistance among the staff?

• What steps can be taken to encourage staff to move from the exploration to the acceptance phase more effectively? How can successes be highlighted to foster a positive attitude towards change?

18.4 Case Discussion 2

Managing Change in Patient Care: Transitioning to Telehealth Services

Scenario:

Brightwood Family Practice plans to introduce telehealth services to improve patient access and streamline care delivery, especially for those who face challenges attending in-person appointments. The clinic staff has mixed feelings about this transition, with some excited about the modern technology and others concerned about its impact on patient relationships and workflow.

Roles:

1. **Clinic Manager (Facilitator):** Responsible for guiding the conversation, addressing concerns, and emphasizing the benefits of telehealth. They will present data on increased patient satisfaction and access to care.

2. **Physician:** The physician expresses concerns about how telehealth might reduce the quality of patient interactions and fears about technology complications affecting patient care.

3. **Nurse:** The nurse is enthusiastic about telehealth, highlighting how it could reduce the number of patients in the clinic and free up time for other essential tasks.

4. **Receptionist:** The receptionist raises practical questions about scheduling and managing appointments and how to handle technical issues that may arise during virtual visits.

5. **Patient Advocate:** This person represents patient perspectives and discusses the benefits of telehealth for patients with mobility issues or those living in remote areas.

Objectives:

- Discuss emotional reactions to the change (denial, resistance, exploration, acceptance) from various staff perspectives.

- To explore effective communication strategies to address concerns and promote acceptance of telehealth services.

- To brainstorm ideas for training and support mechanisms to facilitate the transition to telehealth.

Chapter 19: How to Lead a Change in an Organization

Learning objectives

- Evaluate the effectiveness of leadership strategies in managing change.

- Create a comprehensive change management plan for a healthcare organization.

- Lead a change initiative from conception to implementation and evaluation.

19.1 Leadership Skills for Change

Characteristics of Effective Change Leaders: Vision, Communication, and Emotional Intelligence

Effective change leaders possess several key characteristics that empower them to guide their teams through change successfully:

- **Vision:** Leaders need a sharp vision to inspire and direct their teams. In healthcare, a compelling vision for improved patient outcomes, streamlined workflows, or enhanced safety motivates staff to embrace change.

- **Communication:** Effective communication skills ensure all team members understand the change's goals and benefits. Transparent, ongoing communication helps reduce resistance and encourages buy-in from stakeholders at all levels.

- **Emotional Intelligence:** Leaders who exhibit emotional intelligence can better manage their emotions and empathize with their team members. This skill is especially valuable in healthcare, where changes can evoke anxiety or stress, as it enables leaders to offer understanding and support.

Engaging and Aligning Stakeholders to Support Change Initiatives

Engaging stakeholders—such as clinicians, administrators, and patients—is crucial for the success of any change initiative. Leaders can achieve alignment by involving key stakeholders early in planning, fostering collaboration, and encouraging input and feedback. Aligning stakeholders around shared goals and benefits of the change helps build trust and commitment.

Monitoring, Evaluating, and Adjusting the Change Process

Effective change leaders regularly monitor and evaluate the progress of change initiatives. By setting measurable goals and collecting data, they can assess if the change meets its intended objectives. Leaders must also be prepared to adjust as needed, addressing any emerging challenges or feedback from staff to ensure that the change process stays on track.

Building a Change-Ready Culture

Techniques to Create a Culture of Flexibility and Innovation in Healthcare Teams

Creating a ready-to-ready culture requires cultivating an environment that values flexibility, innovation, and continuous improvement. Techniques include encouraging open communication, supporting creative problem-solving, and recognizing team members who adapt well to change. Leaders can foster a learning culture where staff feel comfortable experimenting with innovative ideas and sharing insights.

Training Programs to Develop Leadership Skills in Managing Change

Ongoing training programs that build leadership skills are essential for creating a workforce capable of managing change. Programs should focus on developing skills in communication, conflict resolution, and adaptability. Providing leadership training in emotional intelligence and strategic planning prepares healthcare leaders to guide teams effectively through change.

19.2 Case Study

Leading Change - From science to societal impact: How one public servant led the charge to make kidney disease a national health issue.

Case Summary

1 - Successful Implementation of Change: Sandeep Patel's leadership in launching KidneyX and the Advancing American Kidney Health Initiative is a prime example of transformative leadership in healthcare. His ability to implement significant changes reflects the core focus of the module.

2 - Impact on Patient Care: Patel's initiatives directly address critical health challenges affecting millions, highlighting how healthcare leaders can drive improvements in patient outcomes and quality of care.

3 - Collaboration Across Sectors: The collaboration between public and private sectors in KidneyX highlights how effective leaders mobilize resources and stakeholders to achieve transformative results, a key theme in the module.

4 - Visionary Leadership: Patel's vision for kidney health and his strategies for inspiring and engaging others exemplify the qualities of transformative leaders, providing a concrete example for students studying effective leadership in healthcare.

Kotter's 8-Step Change Model Applied

1 - Create a Sense of Urgency

Patel recognized the critical health issue posed by kidney disease, noting that millions of Americans rely on dialysis with limited alternatives. By emphasizing the urgency of improving kidney health and discussing the struggles of those affected, he created a compelling reason for stakeholders to engage in change.

2 - Build a Guiding Coalition

Patel mobilized a core group of federal health leaders and stakeholders, including representatives from the private sector. This coalition was essential for championing KidneyX's vision and ensuring that diverse perspectives were represented in the initiative.

3 - Form a Strategic Vision and Initiatives

Patel articulated a sharp vision for the Kidney Innovation Accelerator (KidneyX) as a "moonshot approach" to finding alternatives to dialysis. This vision inspired stakeholders and clarified the initiative's objectives, emphasizing collaboration across sectors.

4 - Communicate the Vision for Buy-In

To gain support, Patel communicated the KidneyX vision in a way that framed the initiative positively, stating it would complement existing efforts rather than criticize them. He engaged in frequent dialogues to build trust and encourage buy-in from those hesitant about open innovation.

5 - Empower Broad-Based Action

Patel encouraged risk-taking and experimentation among stakeholders, demonstrating the benefits of open innovation tools like prize competitions and partnerships. He fostered an environment where innovative ideas could flourish, addressing the cultural inertia in government settings.

6 - Generate Short-Term Wins

As KidneyX began to produce results, such as attracting researchers and funding, these early successes were highlighted to maintain momentum. The support from Congress and media attention helped validate the initiative and encouraged further participation.

7 - Consolidate Gains and Produce More Change

Patel built on the momentum from early successes to expand KidneyX's focus beyond dialysis to improve the organ transplant system. He recognized that continued innovation and adaptation were necessary to address the broader challenges in kidney health.

8 - Anchor New Approaches in the Culture

By institutionalizing the concepts of open innovation and collaboration within HHS and the broader healthcare community, Patel laid the groundwork for sustainable change. He encouraged ongoing dialogue and partnership, ensuring these novel approaches became ingrained in the agency's culture.

Reflection on the Case Study

Patel's approach exemplifies effective change leadership by aligning his vision with stakeholders' needs, fostering a culture of innovation, and demonstrating the potential impact of collaborative efforts. His ability to navigate organizational resistance and inspire others to take risks highlights the importance of commitment and adaptability in leading change initiatives.

19.3 Interactive Activity: Implementing an Electronic Health Record System

Sunrise Medical Centre, a busy urban hospital, has transitioned from paper-based patient records to an electronic health record (EHR) system to improve efficiency and enhance patient care. The leadership team understands that this meaningful change will affect all staff members, from physicians and nurses to administrative personnel. To lead this initiative effectively, the hospital's chief medical officer (CMO) has developed a comprehensive change management plan, which includes identifying key stakeholders across departments, establishing a clear vision for the new EHR system, and communicating its benefits. The CMO conducts meetings to address concerns, allowing staff to share feedback and express their anxieties about the change. A task force of representatives from each department is formed to ensure all perspectives are considered throughout the implementation process. The leadership team regularly monitors the progress of the EHR rollout, using metrics to evaluate its impact on workflow efficiency and patient outcomes while remaining flexible and responsive to staff feedback.

Questions:

1. What leadership strategies did the CMO employ to manage the EHR system change effectively?

2. How did the CMO ensure stakeholders were engaged and aligned with the change initiative?

3. What metrics could be used to evaluate the effectiveness of the EHR system post-implementation?

4. In what ways did the leadership team address staff concerns and anxieties regarding the transition?

5. How can the hospital cultivate a change-ready culture to support future initiatives?

19.4 Interactive Activity: Launching a New Patient Safety Initiative

Green Valley Hospital is experiencing a rise in patient safety incidents, prompting leadership to launch a new patient safety initiative to reduce errors and enhance overall care quality. The hospital's executive team recognizes that successfully implementing this initiative requires a strong leadership approach. The chief nursing officer (CNO) leads in developing a strategic plan emphasizing a sharp vision for patient safety, effective communication strategies, and emotional intelligence in addressing staff concerns. The CNO hosts an all-staff meeting to introduce the initiative, outlining its goals and positive impact on patient care. A feedback mechanism facilitates engagement, allowing staff to voice their thoughts and suggestions. Training sessions are scheduled to equip staff with the necessary skills and knowledge to support the new safety protocols. As the initiative progresses, the CNO regularly evaluates its effectiveness through patient safety data, staff surveys, and incident reports, adjusting as needed to ensure ongoing success.

Questions:

1. What leadership characteristics did the CNO demonstrate to guide the patient safety initiative?

2. How did the CNO facilitate stakeholder engagement and buy-in for the initiative?

3. What methods could the hospital use to monitor and evaluate the effectiveness of the patient safety initiative?

4. How did the CNO address potential resistance from staff regarding the new safety protocols?

5. What steps can Green Valley Hospital take to foster a culture of continuous improvement in patient safety?

19.4 Quick Check

1. What does change in healthcare primarily refer to?

A) A new policy implementation
B) Improving service delivery and patient outcomes
C) Changes in healthcare laws
D) Reducing costs in healthcare?

2. Which of the following is NOT a key concept related to change in healthcare settings?

A) Organizational Change
B) Quality Improvement
C) Financial Management
D) Change Management

3. What is the definition of quality improvement in healthcare?

A) A marketing strategy
B) Systematic efforts to improve healthcare services
C) A new medical technology
D) Patient satisfaction surveys?

4. What does stakeholder engagement involve in the context of change?

A) Limiting feedback to top management
B) Involvement of all parties affected by changes
C) Only engaging healthcare providers
D) Focusing solely on patient feedback?

5. Which trend focuses on tailoring healthcare services to individual patient needs?

A) Telehealth Expansion
B) Value-Based Care
C) Patient-Cantered Care
D) Regulatory Changes

6. What is one of the challenges facing healthcare due to an aging population?

A) Decreased demand for services
B) Increased demand for services and chronic conditions
C) More professionals entering the field
D) Reduction in healthcare disparities

7. How has health information technology advanced healthcare?

A) By eliminating the need for healthcare professionals
B) Through the adoption of electronic health records and data analytics
C) By increasing the number of in-person visits
D) By standardizing all medical procedures?

8. Why is change necessary to improve patient outcomes?

A) To reduce healthcare costs
B) To enhance the quality and safety of patient care
C) To standardize treatments across all facilities
D) To increase the number of healthcare providers.

9. What does value-based care focus on?

A) Fee-for-service models
B) Patient outcomes and cost-efficiency
C) Reducing administrative costs
D) Increasing the number of services provided?

10.What direct benefits were observed at the Ohio State University Comprehensive Cancer Centre?

A) Increased operational costs
B) Improved patient outcomes through enhanced team dynamics
C) Decreased patient satisfaction
D) Lower staffing requirements?

Correct answers:

1 - B

2 - C

3 - B

4 - B

5 - C

6 - B

7 - B

8 - B

9 - B

10-B

Bibliography

1. Bodenheimer, T., & Sinsky, C. (2014). From Triple to Quadruple Aim: Care of the Patient Requires Care of the Provider. Annals of Family Medicine, 12(6), 573-576.

2. Berwick, D. M. (2016). Era 3 for Medicine and Health Care. JAMA, 315(13), 1329-1330.

3. Burch, V. C., & Roberts, L. (2020). Creating change: Kotter's Change Management Model in action. Canadian Medical Education Journal, 11(2), e32-e36. Retrieved from https://journalhosting.ucalgary.ca/index.php/cmej/article/view/76680

4. Burnes, B. (2004). "Kurt Lewin and the Planned Approach to Change: A Re-appraisal." Journal of Management Studies, 41(6), 977-1002.

5. Dixon-Woods, M., et al. (2014). Explaining Michigan's High Hospital Mortality Rates: A Qualitative Study. BMJ Quality & Safety, 23(12), 977-985.

6. Institute for Healthcare Improvement (IHI). (2021). The IHI Triple Aim: Improving the Patient Experience of Care, Improving the Health of Populations, and Reducing the Per Capita Cost of Health Care.

7. Institute of Medicine (IOM). (2015). Measuring the Impact of Interprofessional Education on Collaborative Practice and Patient Outcomes.

8. McKinsey & Company. (2020). Telehealth: A quarter-trillion-dollar post-COVID-19 reality?

9. American Hospital Association (AHA). (2020). The Health Care Workforce and COVID-19: A Summary of the Impact.

10. World Health Organization (WHO). (2016). Framework on Integrated, People-Centred Health Services.

10. Kotter, J. P. (1996). Leading Change. Harvard Business Review Press.

11. Health Affairs. (2020). The Promise of Telehealth for Health Care in the COVID-19 Era and Beyond.

3

Section three:

Marketing in Healthcare

This section introduces marketing concepts and their application in healthcare settings. It explores the unique challenges and opportunities of marketing within the healthcare industry, focusing on ethics, patient engagement, and strategic approaches. Designed for doctors, nurses, physicians, and healthcare professors, this course integrates case studies, real-world examples, and industry research to highlight the importance of marketing in improving patient outcomes, hospital branding, and organizational success. By understanding and applying these marketing principles, healthcare professionals can significantly impact their patients' well-being.

Learning Objectives:

1. Understand the principles of marketing and their application in healthcare.

2. Develop strategies for patient engagement, communication, and retention.

3. Learn ethical and regulatory considerations in healthcare marketing.

4. Explore digital tools and data analytics for effective healthcare marketing.

Chapter 20: Introduction to Healthcare Marketing

20.1 What is Marketing? Philosophy or Process?

Definition and Evolution of Marketing

Marketing is creating, communicating, delivering, and exchanging offerings that have value for customers, clients, partners, and society (American Marketing Association, 2017). The concept of marketing has evolved over decades:

1. Production Era: Focus on mass production and efficiency.

2. Sales Era: Emphasis on aggressive sales tactics.

3. Marketing Era: Shift toward understanding and fulfilling customer needs.

4. Relationship Era: Building long-term relationships with customers.

Marketing as a Philosophy vs. a Process

- Philosophy: Marketing as a mindset prioritizes understanding and meeting customer needs. Kotler and Keller (2016) argue that this philosophy promotes customer-centricity and long-term value creation.

- Process: It involves specific steps such as market research, segmentation, targeting, and positioning. Lamb et al. (2021) state that marketing integrates strategy, execution, and feedback loops.

20.2 Overview of Marketing in Healthcare

Defining Healthcare Marketing

Healthcare marketing refers to strategies and practices for communicating and delivering value to patients, promoting healthcare services, and improving patient engagement (Thomas, 2008).

Unique Challenges in Marketing Healthcare Services

1. Regulatory Constraints

• Healthcare marketers must comply with stringent regulations such as HIPAA (Health Insurance Portability and Accountability Act) and GDPR (General Data Protection Regulation).

• These laws govern how patient data is collected, stored, and used, adding complexity to digital marketing strategies like email campaigns and targeted ads.

2. Complex Decision-Making

• Patients often base healthcare decisions on trust, emotional factors, and peer recommendations rather than cost or convenience.

• Marketing must address these emotional triggers while providing logical, evidence-based reassurances about the quality of care.

3. Sensitivity of Healthcare Information

• Patient health data is overly sensitive, and any mishandling can erode trust and result in legal penalties.

• Marketing messages must be carefully crafted to avoid being invasive or triggering negative emotions while respecting patients' vulnerabilities.

4. Diverse Patient Demographics

• Healthcare providers serve many patients with different languages, cultural backgrounds, and healthcare literacy levels.

• Marketers must create inclusive, accessible content tailored to the unique needs of each demographic group.

5. Intangible and Experiential Nature of Services

• Unlike products, healthcare services are intangible and cannot be experienced beforehand, making it hard for patients to assess quality.

• Marketing must focus on storytelling, testimonials, and visual content to build confidence in the service offerings.

6. Long Decision-Making Cycles

• Healthcare decisions often involve multiple stakeholders, including family members, primary care providers, and insurance companies.

• This prolonged decision-making process requires consistent follow-ups and educational content to guide patients through their journey.

7. Increased Competition in the Healthcare Market

• The healthcare industry has seen a surge in competitors, including telemedicine providers, wellness apps, and alternative care services.

• Standing out in this crowded market requires innovative marketing strategies and a strong emphasis on unique value propositions.

8. Rapid Technological Advancements

• With rapid technological advancements in healthcare, such as AI-driven diagnostics, telehealth, and wearable health devices, it's crucial for healthcare professionals to stay updated. This proactive approach keeps them abreast of the latest trends, helps them educate patients, and differentiates these technologies in the market, adding value to their promotional efforts.

• Educating patients and differentiating these technologies in the market adds complexity to promotional efforts.

9. Crisis and Reputation Management

• Negative reviews, malpractice lawsuits, or public health crises can quickly damage a healthcare brand's reputation.

• Marketers must develop robust crisis communication plans and proactively manage online reputations through transparent and empathetic messaging.

10. Budget Constraints

• Many healthcare organizations operate on tight budgets, minimal practices, and non-profits.

• Marketers must find cost-effective solutions, like leveraging organic social media or local partnerships, to maximize impact without overspending.

20.3 Importance of Marketing for Healthcare Professionals

Patient Psychology and Decision-Making Factors

Patients are not solely influenced by the technical aspects of care when selecting a healthcare provider. Emotional factors, such as trust and perceived empathy, play a significant role in shaping their decisions. For many, the assurance of being understood and cared for often outweighs other considerations like cost or convenience. Trust in a provider is built through consistent, transparent communication and the ability to address patient concerns effectively.

Another critical factor is perceived competence. Patients are likelier to choose a provider who demonstrates expertise, professionalism, and reliability. Visible quality markers, such as certifications, accreditations, or the provider's success stories and case studies, can influence this perception.

Word-of-mouth recommendations and peer influences further shape patient choices. Testimonials, online reviews, and referrals from trusted individuals like family members or friends often hold more weight than traditional advertising. Patients in the digital information age do extensive research, looking for providers who align with their values and offer the best outcomes.

Building Trust and Reputation in a Competitive Market

Trust is the cornerstone of patient loyalty in a highly competitive healthcare landscape. Effective marketing goes beyond simply promoting services; it focuses on creating genuine connections with the community. Content marketing, such as educational blogs, videos, and patient success stories, helps position providers as thought leaders and trusted advisors.

Engaging with the community through health awareness campaigns, local events, or partnerships with non-profits reinforces a provider's commitment to public welfare, further building trust. Consistency in messaging, branding, and the quality of care strengthens the provider's reputation over time.

A compelling reputation attracts new patients and retains existing ones by fostering loyalty. When patients feel confident in their choice, they are more likely to return for future needs and recommend the provider to others. A provider's reputation becomes its most powerful marketing tool, driving sustainable growth and enhancing its standing in the market.

20.4 The Impact of Marketing on Healthcare Outcomes

A Gradual Process Requiring Consistency

Marketing in healthcare is not about instant results; it is a long-term strategy that builds trust and credibility over time. Consistency in messaging helps create a recognizable and dependable brand identity, which fosters patient confidence. Repeated exposure to clear, empathetic, and relevant messages reassures patients of the provider's commitment to their well-being.

Prolonged Influence on Patient Behaviour

Strategic marketing does more than attract patients; it influences long-term behaviors and fosters loyalty. Educational campaigns, for example, play a critical role in improving health literacy by giving patients the knowledge they need to make informed decisions about their health. When patients understand their conditions, treatment options, and preventive measures, they are more likely to engage proactively with their care.

Marketing can also shape adherence to treatment plans and encourage routine healthcare practices, such as regular check-ups or screenings. By framing healthcare as a continuous journey rather than a one-time interaction, marketing helps patients view their relationship with a provider as an ongoing partnership.

20.5 Quick Check

1. Which of the following best describes marketing as a process?

A) A customer-focused mindset

B) A series of steps involving research, segmentation, and feedback loops

C) A set of activities aimed at aggressive sales tactics

D) A focus on mass production and efficiency

2. Which of the following is a unique challenge in healthcare marketing?

A) Low patient turnover

B) Regulatory constraints like HIPAA and GDPR

C) Intangible nature of physical products

D) Limited technological advancements in the field

3. What emotional factor most likely influences a patient's decision when choosing a healthcare provider?

A) The clinic's location and proximity to their home

B) Perceived empathy and trust in the provider

C) The cost of the healthcare services

D) The variety of services offered by the provider

4. Which marketing tactic can help healthcare providers build trust
in their services?

A) Aggressive sales tactics

B) Educational content and patient success stories

C) Focusing on high discounts and offers

D) Offering the lowest prices in the market

5. What is the primary goal of marketing in healthcare?

A) To create immediate sales and revenue

B) To build long-term trust, relationships, and educate patients

C) To highlight the affordability of healthcare services

D) To focus solely on acquiring new patients

Correct answers

1- A

2- B

3- B

4- B

5- B

20.6 Healthcare marketing case study: 27x more patient bookings

Background

A Health-tech startup offered at-home primary care services to affluent patients seeking convenience in overcrowded clinics. While operational costs were high, their in-house marketing efforts were costly and ineffective. They spent $48 per new patient and relied on deep discounts that eroded profitability.

Challenges

- High operational costs with low patient acquisition efficiency.

- Ineffective use of digital ads, leading to unsustainable growth.

- There is a need to build trust and a predictable acquisition channel.

Solutions

1. Shift in Advertising Strategy

- Moved budgets from underperforming social media ads to Google Search Ads targeting healthcare-related keywords (e.g., "home care doctors").

- Identified opportunities to reach patients looking for competitors or alternative care.

2. Optimizing Campaigns

• Tested different targeting strategies and refined ad copy using a structured "gladiator battle" approach to isolate high-performing ideas.

• Created new ad funnels to tap into less prominent but promising keywords, balancing cost per patient and volume.

Results

• Reduced patient acquisition cost from $48 to $19.

• Increased new patient bookings by 27x, reaching near-full capacity.

• Eliminated the need for discounts, improving margins and patient quality.

• Established a reliable and scalable patient acquisition system.

Discussion Questions

1. How does this case reflect the process of creating, delivering, and exchanging offerings with value for patients?

2. In what ways did the startup demonstrate customer-centric marketing   practices?

3. How did the startup address the challenge of trust and emotional decision-making in patient acquisition?

4. What steps were taken to balance budget constraints while achieving   effective   results?

5. Why did the startup need to avoid deep discounts in its marketing strategy?

6. How did optimizing campaigns contribute to building trust and long-term reputation?

7. What role did marketing play in shaping patient behavior and improving healthcare outcomes in this case?

8. How does establishing a predictable patient acquisition channel impact the sustainability of healthcare services?

Source: https://healthtechhippo.com/healthcare-marketing-case-study/

Chapter 21: Module 2: Sales vs. Marketing in Healthcare

21.1 Understanding the Difference Between Sales and Marketing in Healthcare

Sales and marketing in healthcare serve distinct yet interconnected purposes. Marketing focuses on creating awareness, building trust, and attracting potential patients by emphasizing the value and benefits of healthcare services. It employs content marketing, public relations, and digital campaigns to nurture a broad audience over time.

On the other hand, selling in healthcare involves direct interactions between healthcare providers or sales agents and potential patients. According to the study "Personal Selling in Health and Medicine: Using Sales Agents to Engage Audiences" (2020), personal selling is particularly effective in addressing the complex decision-making process of healthcare consumers, as it provides tailored communication and builds trust.

The key distinction lies in their objectives: marketing adopts a long-term strategy to develop relationships and establish trust, while sales focus on short-term actions that drive results. In healthcare, integrating both functions ensures a seamless patient experience, enhancing satisfaction and long-term engagement.

The Role of Services Marketing in Building Long-Term Patient Relationships

As patients increasingly take an active role in healthcare decisions due to escalating costs and greater awareness, services marketing has become essential for fostering long-term relationships. Corbin, Kelley, and Schwartz (2001) emphasize that healthcare professionals and organizations can use proven service marketing principles to enhance patient satisfaction and loyalty while maintaining financial viability in a competitive market.

Key Concepts in Services Marketing for Patient Relationships

1. Service Quality and the Zone of Tolerance:

Patients' perceptions of healthcare services often fall within a "zone of tolerance," where expectations are met or exceeded. Effective marketing ensures that healthcare providers consistently deliver quality care within this zone, reinforcing trust and reliability, which are essential for lasting relationships.

2. Consumer Satisfaction Levels:

Patient satisfaction is about meeting clinical needs and addressing emotional and service-related factors like communication, empathy, and convenience. Healthcare organizations prioritizing these elements in their marketing strategies see higher retention rates and stronger patient-provider bonds.

3. Branding of Services:

Branding in healthcare involves more than visual identity; it reflects the organization's values, quality of care, and patient-centric focus. A well-defined brand fosters trust and differentiates the provider in a crowded market, encouraging patients to return and recommend services.

4. Encouraging Patient Participation:

Marketing efforts that empower patients to participate actively in healthcare decisions through education shared decision-making, and easy access to resources strengthen their sense of ownership and loyalty to the provider.

5. Service Recovery Strategies:

Mistakes or service lapses can erode patient trust if not addressed effectively. A robust service recovery framework ensures that concerns are resolved promptly and empathetically, often turning negative experiences into opportunities to strengthen relationships.

21.2 Integrating Sales Tactics with Healthcare Marketing Strategies

Combining sales and marketing strategies creates a unified approach that maximizes patient satisfaction and outcomes. Sales tactics can be integrated with marketing efforts by:

- Leveraging Data Analytics: Marketing data on patient demographics and behavior can inform personalized sales pitches.

- Cross-functional Training: Educating sales teams on the values and messaging promoted in marketing ensures consistency in patient interactions.

- Feedback Loops: Insights from sales interactions can help refine marketing strategies, address gaps, and improve messaging.

This integration aligns both functions to deliver excellent patient care while driving growth and trust in the healthcare organization.

21.3 Case Discussion: Should Sales and Marketing Report to the Same Manager?

Scenario:

In many organizations, Sales and Marketing are two distinct departments with different objectives and strategies. Marketing focuses on creating brand awareness, generating leads, and driving customer interest, while Sales concentrates on closing deals and maintaining client relationships. A new organizational proposal suggests that both departments should report to the same manager—the Marketing Director.

Pros of Having Sales and Marketing Report to the Same Manager:

1. Improved Alignment: A unified leadership structure ensures that both teams work toward common objectives. With shared goals, there is less chance of miscommunication or conflicting strategies.

2. Better Communication: A single manager can ensure that both teams know each other's progress and challenges. Regular meetings and updates between Sales and Marketing can promote smoother collaboration.

3. Streamlined Strategy: With one manager overseeing both functions, marketing campaigns can be designed with sales objectives in mind, resulting in more targeted and effective lead generation and conversion.

4. Resource Efficiency: A unified management structure might lead to a more efficient allocation of resources, such as budgets and personnel, as the manager has visibility into the needs of both teams.

Cons of Having Sales and Marketing Report to the Same Manager:

1. Potential Overload: The Marketing Director may struggle to effectively manage both functions, leading to burnout or insufficient attention to either Sales or Marketing priorities.

2. Conflict of Interests: Sales teams may prioritize immediate results and revenue, while Marketing teams may focus on long-term brand building and lead nurturing. A single manager could struggle to balance these sometimes conflicting priorities.

3. Lack of Specialization: Sales and Marketing have different skill sets and expertise. Combining them under one leader may dilute the effectiveness of both teams, as the manager may not be able to address the unique needs of each department fully.

4. Resistance to Change: Sales and Marketing may have established cultures and ways of working that are difficult to change. Aligning these teams may face resistance, potentially leading to inefficiencies or disengagement.

Discussion Question:

Given the pros and cons, should Sales and Marketing report to the same manager?

What is your opinion, and how might the organization ensure that both departments work effectively together, even if they are led separately?

21.4 Key Performance Indicators for Healthcare Marketing

KPIs in Marketing

Measuring the success of healthcare marketing campaigns requires using specific Key Performance Indicators (KPIs) that align with organizational goals. Common healthcare marketing KPIs include:

• Patient Acquisition Cost (PAC): The cost of acquiring a new patient through marketing efforts.

• Lead Conversion Rate: The percentage of leads generated by marketing that convert into actual patients.

• Patient Retention Rate: The proportion of patients who continue using the provider's services over time.

• Engagement Metrics: Metrics such as website traffic, social media interactions, and email open rates that measure the reach and impact of marketing campaigns.

• Return on Investment (ROI): The financial return generated from marketing efforts compared to the resources invested.

By regularly tracking these KPIs, healthcare providers can refine their strategies to maximize effectiveness and ensure alignment with patient needs and organizational objectives.

KIPI's in Marketing

Key Intangible Performance Indicators (KIPIs) in marketing focus on measuring the less quantifiable aspects of a brand's performance, such as customer loyalty, perception, and emotional engagement. Nguyen et al. (2016) propose six fuzzy key performance indicators (KPIs) that measure customer retention and loyalty within a company's portfolio. These KPIs link market orientation (MO) and customer value to sustainable sales growth. Here are the six indicators outlined in the study:

1. Market Orientation (MO): This represents how effectively the company gathers, shares, and responds to market intelligence, influencing customer alignment and retention.

2. Customer Orientation (CO): Measures the degree to which the company prioritizes understanding and fulfilling customer needs through its processes and interactions.

3. Degree of Customer Orientation Value of the Sales Force: This measure focuses on how well the sales team aligns its approach to delivering value that resonates with customers.

4. Innovation Capability: Evaluate the company's ability to innovate in products, services, or processes to enhance customer satisfaction and loyalty.

5. Lifetime Value (LTV): This assesses the predicted net profit from a customer's entire relationship with the company, helping to gauge the importance of long-term retention.

6. Customer Service Quality: Measures perceived quality in service delivery, responsiveness, and problem resolution, critical for retaining customers.

21.5 Leveraging Intangibles for Competitive Edge

KIPs emphasize the critical role of intangible assets such as leadership, innovation, reputation, and employee satisfaction. These factors are more complex to quantify yet pivotal for long-term organizational success (Ng & Kee, 2011). Many KIPs, though intangible, are also inherently fuzzy, requiring innovative methods to measure their impact. For instance:

Leadership: Guides strategic decisions, shaping tangible (product innovation) and intangible (brand reputation) outcomes.

Innovation: Fuels creativity and agility, impacting both internal processes and external perceptions.

Employee Satisfaction: Intangibly drives customer satisfaction, retention, and loyalty.

Reputation: Acts as a multiplier, influencing customer loyalty, market positioning, and long-term success.

Measuring the Long-term Impact of KIPIs on Brand Success

To measure the long-term impact of intangible indicators on your brand's success, start by setting up tools that track real-world results.

For example:

1. Customer Feedback Systems: Use surveys, reviews, or Net Promoter Scores (NPS) to assess satisfaction and loyalty regularly. These insights highlight how your brand resonates over time.

2. Brand Awareness Metrics: Monitor online mentions, social media engagement, and search trends to see how your brand stays top-of-mind in the market.

3. Sales Data and Retention Rates: Analyse customer lifetime value and repeat purchases to connect customer retention with your branding and marketing efforts.

4. Innovation Tracking: Log how new products or services improve market share or customer interest—linking innovation directly to sales performance.

5. Market Position Analysis: Using competitor benchmarking to measure leadership or service quality can boost your standing against rivals.

21.6 Quick Check

1. What is the primary objective of marketing in healthcare?

A) To close sales and generate immediate revenue

B) To build brand awareness, trust, and long-term relationships with patients

C) To focus on immediate sales outcomes and profit generation

D) To only promote healthcare products to healthcare professionals

2. How does selling in healthcare differ from marketing?

A) Selling focuses on long-term relationships, while marketing targets immediate transactions

B) Selling involves direct, personalized communication, while marketing uses broad strategies to attract potential patients

C) Selling uses mass communication channels while marketing targets niche audiences

D) Selling focuses on creating awareness, while marketing involves closing deals

3. What is a key distinction between marketing and sales in healthcare?

A) Marketing seeks short-term profits, while sales aim for long-term patient retention

B) Marketing focuses on customer relationships, while sales focus on one-time transactions

C) Marketing focuses on long-term trust-building, while sales focus on short-term revenue generation

D) Marketing handles customer care, while sales are responsible for financial transactions

4. Which of the following is NOT a key concept in services marketing for patient relationships?

A) Service quality within the zone of tolerance

B) Building trust through personalized healthcare

C) Creating immediate sales through discounts

D) Empowering patient participation in healthcare decisions

5. What is the 'zone of tolerance' in services marketing?

A) The range of acceptable prices for healthcare services

B) The difference between patient expectations and actual service delivery

C) The minimum threshold for patient satisfaction

D) A method for determining patient loyalty

6. Which of the following is an example of integrating sales tactics with healthcare marketing strategies?

A) Using data analytics to personalize sales pitches based on patient demographics

B) Implementing random outreach campaigns without focusing on patient data

C) Separating marketing and sales activities to focus on short-term profits

D) Reducing focus on patient feedback to increase immediate sales

7. What is a key healthcare marketing performance indicator (KPI)?

A) Website traffic, social media interactions, and email open rates

B) Patient Acquisition Cost (PAC) and Lead Conversion Rate

C) Return on Investment (ROI) for healthcare campaigns

D) All of the above

8. What is the primary focus of Key Intangible Performance Indicators (KIPIs) in healthcare marketing?

A) Measuring customer acquisition costs

B) Measuring customer loyalty, brand perception, and emotional engagement

C) Tracking sales volume and lead generation

D) Evaluating operational costs and profit margins

9. What does the Lifetime Value (LTV) metric assess in healthcare marketing?

A) The cost of acquiring a new patient

B) The predicted net profit from a patient over their entire relationship with the healthcare provider

C) The percentage of leads that convert into actual patients

D) The number of patients served each time

10. What is the primary purpose of a Service Recovery Strategy in healthcare marketing?

A) To lower service costs for patients

B) To handle negative feedback and convert negative experiences into positive ones

C) To increase the volume of sales and patient turnover

D) To create brand awareness through digital marketing channels

Correct Answers:

1- B

2- B

3- C

4- C

5- B

6- A

7- D

8- B

9- B

10- B

21.7 Case Study: Cleveland Clinic's Content and Patient Outreach Strategy

Cleveland Clinic, a nonprofit healthcare organization, is renowned for integrating sales and marketing strategies to drive patient engagement and improve outcomes. It employs a robust content marketing approach, including its award-winning Health Essentials blog and podcasts, featuring expert advice, health tips, and patient success stories. These efforts build trust, educate audiences, and establish the clinic as a thought leader in healthcare.

In 2022, Cleveland Clinic adopted a marketing-sales integration strategy to streamline its patient acquisition process:

1. Data Utilization: Marketing teams used CRM tools and analytics to segment patients based on needs and engagement history, creating targeted outreach campaigns.

2. Personalized Sales Approach: Sales teams utilized this data to engage patients with tailored communication, offering specific services aligned with their preferences and health concerns.

3. Feedback Loop: Sales insights were fed into marketing to refine messaging and improve future campaigns.

Results:

- 3 million monthly blog visitors, many of whom became patients.

- A 15% increase in appointment bookings attributed to targeted campaigns.

- Enhanced patient trust and satisfaction scores, with 90% of surveyed patients citing the Clinic's educational resources as a factor in choosing their services.

Discussion Questions:

1. Understanding Differences: How did Cleveland Clinic's marketing strategies differ from its sales tactics in achieving its goals?

2. Services Marketing in Relationships: In what ways did Cleveland Clinic's content efforts contribute to building long-term patient relationships?

3. Integration Benefits: What benefits did Cleveland Clinic achieve by integrating its sales and marketing functions?

4. Challenges and Solutions: What challenges might Cleveland Clinic have faced in implementing this integration, and how could they address them?

5. Key Metrics: What Key Performance Indicators (KPIs) would you recommend tracking to measure the success of Cleveland Clinic's integrated approach?

https://www.growthganik.com/blog/healthcare-marketing-case-studies/

Chapter 23: Healthcare as a Services Product

23.1 The 7Ps of Marketing in Healthcare

The 7Ps of marketing—product, Price, Place, Promotion, People, Process, and Physical Evidence—are essential elements that help healthcare providers craft strategies to enhance patient satisfaction and ensure high-quality service delivery. These seven elements are interconnected, creating a comprehensive healthcare service marketing framework.

1. Product: Healthcare services are intangible and rely on the expertise of healthcare professionals, technology, and the physical environment in which care is provided. The "product" in healthcare includes various services, such as treatments, consultations, diagnostics, and wellness programs. Hospitals and healthcare providers must ensure that the offerings meet patient expectations and needs.

2. Price: Healthcare pricing strategies must consider patient perceptions of value, affordability, and insurance coverage. A study on hospitals in Jeddah (Khalaf et al., 2013) found that while pricing is crucial, it did not significantly impact patient satisfaction, suggesting that service quality and trust play a more significant role in patient decision-making.

3. Place: The accessibility of healthcare services, including geographic location, the convenience of appointment scheduling, and online access to care (telemedicine), determines a patient's ability to seek and continue care.

4. Promotion: Promoting healthcare services through advertising, public relations, and patient education fosters awareness and attracts potential patients. Effective promotion includes traditional advertising, word-of-mouth, and digital marketing to build trust and credibility.

5. People: The staff, including healthcare professionals, support staff, and administrators, all play a critical role in service delivery. Patients evaluate care quality based on their interactions with healthcare staff. Training staff to be empathetic, knowledgeable, and responsive is crucial for building long-term patient relationships.

6. Process: Healthcare processes encompass everything from the efficiency of booking appointments to the quality of post-treatment care. Smooth processes enhance the patient experience, reduce waiting times, and ensure patient satisfaction, which is critical for hospital success. A study by Khalaf et al. (2013) found that process strategies significantly impact patient satisfaction in healthcare.

7. Physical Evidence: In healthcare, physical evidence includes the hospital or clinic environment, facilities, technology, and branding materials such as signage or brochures. The physical appearance of healthcare facilities and the cleanliness of the environment significantly impact the perception of care quality.

These seven components must work cohesively to provide a high-quality, patient-centered experience. Integrating all these elements leads to greater patient satisfaction, increased loyalty, and better hospital performance.

23.2 Managing the Intangible Aspects of Healthcare Services

Unlike physical products, healthcare services are intangible, making patients skeptical about their value until they experience them firsthand. To manage this, healthcare providers must focus on creating trust and transparency. Effective service marketing should emphasize the quality of care, personalized attention, and the overall patient experience. This involves ensuring that all in-person, via phone, or online interactions are positive, reassuring, and informative.Focusing on brand reputation and quality assurance can mitigate the intangibility of healthcare services, helping patients feel confident about their healthcare decisions even before they receive care.

SERVQUAL and Healthcare Service Quality

Introduction to the SERVQUAL Model

The SERVQUAL model is a widely adopted tool for evaluating service quality. It assesses the gap between patient expectations and the actual service delivered. In healthcare, this model helps identify the factors that influence patient satisfaction and how services can be improved. The SERVQUAL model includes five key dimensions:

1. Reliability: The ability to consistently perform healthcare services as promised.

2. Assurance: The professionalism and confidence of healthcare staff ensure that patients feel safe and trust their care providers.

3. Tangibles: The physical appearance of healthcare facilities, staff, and equipment, which reflects the quality of service.

4. Empathy: How healthcare providers show care and individualized attention to patients.

5. Responsiveness: The willingness and ability of staff to respond to patient needs promptly and effectively.

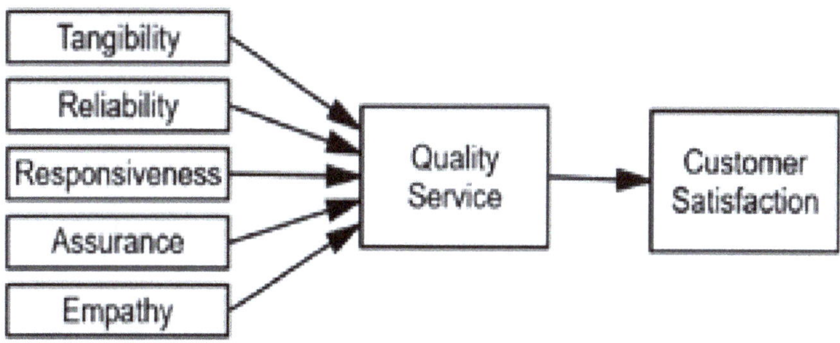

The SERVQUAL Model Source: Adopted from Parasuraman et al. (1988)

Measuring Service Quality in Healthcare Institutions

Healthcare providers can use SERVQUAL surveys to gather feedback on each of these dimensions, helping them identify areas for improvement. Healthcare institutions can fine-tune their operations, training, and environment to meet patient expectations and enhance satisfaction by understanding patients' perceptions.

Identifying and Addressing Service Quality Gaps in Healthcare

Service gaps occur when patient expectations are disconnected from their experiences. Identifying these gaps through tools like SERVQUAL surveys enables healthcare institutions to address issues proactively, ensuring better patient outcomes and satisfaction. For example, improving response times, enhancing patient communication, or upgrading physical facilities can help close service quality gaps.

23.3 The Role of Service Touchpoints in Healthcare

Understanding Service Touchpoints in Healthcare

A service touchpoint is any interaction between the patient and the healthcare provider. These touchpoints are pivotal moments in the patient journey, influencing their overall perception of care. Touchpoints include booking appointments, interacting with administrative staff, seeing a healthcare provider, and even post-treatment follow-up.

Mapping Patient Journey Touchpoints

Healthcare providers can map the patient journey by identifying physical (e.g., in-office visits and hospital interactions) and digital touchpoints (e.g., online consultations, mobile apps, or patient portals). Analyzing these touchpoints enables healthcare providers to identify bottlenecks and areas for improvement, ultimately enhancing the patient experience.

Enhancing Patient Experience Through Service Touchpoints

Optimizing service touchpoints ensures that each interaction is as smooth and efficient as possible. For example, ensuring patients have easy access to appointment scheduling, reducing waiting times, providing clear instructions, and following up post-treatment are all key strategies for improving the patient experience.

The Importance of Frontstage vs. Backstage in Healthcare Services

As Akob et al. (2021) highlight, frontstage refers to the visible aspects of service delivery that patients directly interact with, such as consultations, waiting rooms, and staff communication. In contrast, backstage refers to behind-the-scenes activities, such as administrative processes, data management, and internal coordination, which ensure the service is delivered efficiently. Practical front and backstage operations integration is essential for high service quality and patient satisfaction.

23.4 Quick Check

1. Which of the following is NOT one of the 7Ps of marketing in healthcare?

a) Product
b) Price
c) Process
d) Profit

2. In healthcare services, which element of the 7Ps focuses on the expertise of healthcare professionals and the physical environment?

a) Price
b) Product
c) People
d) Promotion

3. According to the study by Khalaf et al. (2013), which factor was found to have the most significant impact on patient satisfaction in healthcare?

a) Price
b) Process
c) Promotion
d) People

4. Which of the following can be mitigated by focusing on the intangibility of healthcare services?

a) Brand reputation and quality assurance
b) Lower prices
c) Availability of physical evidence
d) Over-promotion

5. Which of the following is NOT one of the five key dimensions of the SERVQUAL model?

a) Reliability
b) Assurance
c) Empathy
d) Efficiency

6. What is the purpose of using SERVQUAL surveys in healthcare?

a) To measure patient demographics
b) To identify areas for service improvement based on patient expectations
c) To track marketing ROI
d) To assess the financial performance of the institution

7. In the SERVQUAL model, which dimension refers to the ability of healthcare staff to perform services as promised?

a) Assurance
b) Empathy
c) Reliability
d) Tangibles

8. Which of the following best describes a 'service touchpoint' in healthcare?

a) A single marketing campaign targeting new patients
b) Any interaction between the patient and the healthcare provider
c) The quality of medical equipment used in treatments
d) The cost of healthcare services

9. What is the role of 'frontstage' in healthcare service delivery?

a) It refers to the administrative tasks behind the scenes.
b) It refers to the visible aspects of service delivery that patients interact with.
c) It refers to the pricing strategies of the healthcare provider.
d) It refers to the healthcare provider's internal data management systems.

10. Which of the following is an example of a 'backstage' activity in healthcare services?

a) A consultation with a doctor
b) Patient Registration
c) Data management and internal coordination
d) post-treatment follow-up

11. What is the primary benefit of mapping the patient journey touchpoints in healthcare?

a) It helps in improving the healthcare provider's marketing budget.
b) It helps identify bottlenecks and areas for service improvement.
c) It tracks patient compliance with medical treatments.
d) It measures the effectiveness of healthcare staff training.

12. Which of the following is NOT a key strategy for enhancing the patient experience through service touchpoints?

a) Ensuring easy access to appointment scheduling
b) Reducing waiting times
c) Providing clear instructions
d) Increasing healthcare prices

Correct answers

1- a

2- b

3- b

4- a

5- d

6- b

7- c

8- b

9- b

10-c

11- b

12- d

23.5 Case Study: Halton Healthcare's Behind-the-Scenes Campaign

Halton Healthcare recognized that many patients perceive medical institutions as impersonal and intimidating, often leading to hesitancy in seeking consultations. To address this, they launched a creative campaign highlighting the human side of their operations.

The campaign included videos highlighting daily activities at the hospital, such as doctors at work, kitchen staff preparing meals, and logistical staff managing operations—these behind-the-scenes glimpses aimed to foster a sense of warmth and approachability.

The initiative succeeded in reshaping patient perceptions. Patients began engaging actively with the content, sharing positive feedback, and commenting on details like their favorite hospital meals, such as the praised chicken soup. This effort enhanced the hospital's image and encouraged more individuals to feel comfortable accessing its services.

Discussion Questions:

Module 3: Healthcare as a Service Product

1. 7Ps of Marketing in Healthcare:

• How did Halton Healthcare incorporate the 7Ps of marketing—Product, People, Process, and Physical Evidence—into its campaign?

• What promotional strategies were most effective in changing perceptions of their services?

2. Managing the Intangible Aspects of Healthcare Services:

• How did the campaign address the intangible nature of healthcare services?

• What role did transparency play in building trust and reducing patient skepticism?

3. SERVQUAL and Healthcare Service Quality:

• Which SERVQUAL dimensions (Reliability, Assurance, Tangibles, Empathy, Responsiveness) were most evident in Halton Healthcare's campaign?

• How could they measure the impact of these efforts on service quality perceptions?

4. The Role of Service Touchpoints in Healthcare:

• How did the behind-the-scenes videos serve as effective touchpoints in the patient journey?

• What other touchpoints could Halton Healthcare optimize to enhance the patient experience?

5. Frontstage vs. Backstage in Healthcare Services:

• How did Halton Healthcare leverage backstage operations to improve the frontstage patient experience?

• What lessons can other healthcare organizations learn from this balance of visibility?

https://www.yumyumvideos.com/blog/healthcare-marketing-case-studies/

Chapter 24: Value Creation in Healthcare Context

24.1 Understanding Value in Healthcare Marketing

Defining Value from Patient and Provider Perspectives

In the healthcare context, patients and providers perceive value differently. For patients, value often stems from service quality, personalized care, and outcomes. It is not only about the cost of treatment but also the emotional, psychological, and physical benefits of the healthcare services they receive. From a provider's perspective, value is about delivering high-quality care efficiently, enhancing patient satisfaction, and achieving positive health outcomes while optimizing resources and maintaining financial sustainability. Both perspectives must align to ensure that value is created in a way that meets the needs of patients while ensuring the viability of healthcare organizations (Çağlıyor, Tosun & Uray, 2022).

Examining Value's Role in Enhancing Patient Satisfaction and Organizational Success

Value is central to both patient satisfaction and organizational success. When patients feel they receive high-quality care responsive to their needs, they are more likely to be satisfied, return for future care, and recommend the provider to others. This enhances the provider's reputation, loyalty, and patient retention, key drivers of organizational success. Organizations that successfully create value for patients are more likely to achieve financial success, operational efficiency, and a competitive advantage in the healthcare market.

24.2 Value-Driven Strategies in Healthcare Marketing

Patient-Cantered Care and Engagement

Patient-centered care places the patient at the core of the healthcare process. Engaging patients in their care decisions, maintaining clear communication, and offering personalized services contribute to a higher perception of value. By actively involving patients in their treatment plans, healthcare providers can foster better relationships and positive experiences, increasing satisfaction and loyalty. This approach improves patient outcomes and builds trust, making patients feel more valued.

Value-Based Marketing and Messaging

Value-based marketing focuses on communicating the most essential benefits and outcomes to patients rather than simply promoting services or products. Messaging should highlight how the healthcare provider can improve patient quality of life, enhance well-being, and deliver outcomes that align with patient values. This approach resonates with patients looking for healthcare providers that prioritize quality over quantity and offer services tailored to individual needs. Value-based messaging also helps healthcare organizations differentiate themselves in a competitive market.

Adopting Technology and Innovation

The integration of technology in healthcare is a critical driver of value creation. Innovations like telemedicine, electronic health records, patient portals, and AI-driven diagnostics enhance operational efficiency and improve patient experiences. By adopting these technologies, healthcare providers can offer more convenient, timely, and accurate care, increasing patient satisfaction and trust. Additionally, technology enables healthcare organizations to streamline operations, reducing costs and improving service delivery.

Focus on Preventive Care and Health Management

Preventive care and health management initiatives, such as wellness programs, screenings, and lifestyle coaching, can significantly improve patient outcomes and reduce healthcare costs. By shifting the focus from reactive treatment to proactive health management, healthcare providers add value by helping patients maintain better long-term health. This approach also empowers patients to take control of their health, leading to better engagement and more favorable outcomes.

Enhancing Operational Efficiency

Operational efficiency is key to delivering value in healthcare. Efficient resource management, optimized patient flow, and adequate staff coordination reduce wait times, lower costs, and improve service delivery. Healthcare organizations focusing on improving operations are better positioned to provide high-quality care without overburdening their budgets. This efficiency translates to better patient experiences, benefitting from timely care and reduced costs.

Developing a Skilled and Engaged Workforce

A skilled and engaged workforce is essential for delivering value in healthcare. When healthcare professionals are well-trained, motivated, and committed to patient care, they are better equipped to provide high-quality services. Staff engagement, including ongoing training and professional development, is key to ensuring that healthcare workers meet evolving patient needs and deliver exceptional care. A positive work environment contributes to better patient-provider relationships, which are integral to value creation.

Sustainability and Long-Term Value

Building sustainable practices is essential for the environment and long-term organizational health. Sustainable healthcare practices can include resource conservation, reducing waste, and implementing green technologies. These efforts reduce costs and improve public perception, aligning with patients' growing interest in environmental responsibility. Additionally, sustainability fosters long-term relationships with patients by demonstrating a commitment to community welfare and future generations.

Data-Driven Decision-Making

Data-driven decision-making is crucial in modern healthcare marketing. Healthcare organizations can identify trends, predict patient needs, and tailor their marketing strategies by leveraging patient data. This enables providers to offer personalized care, improve patient engagement, and optimize service delivery. Data-driven insights also allow healthcare organizations to measure the effectiveness of their marketing efforts, making it possible to refine strategies and increase their impact over time.

24.3 Sustainability and Long-Term Value

Building Sustainable Practices that Benefit Both Patients and the Organization

Sustainable healthcare practices benefit the environment, help reduce operational costs, enhance service delivery, and build a reputation for responsibility. By adopting sustainable healthcare practices, such as reducing energy consumption, sourcing eco-friendly products, and minimizing waste, healthcare organizations create value for patients and the organization. Patients are increasingly drawn to organizations prioritizing sustainability, which drives loyalty and satisfaction.

Fostering Long-Term Relationships through Consistent and Reliable Service Quality

Consistent and reliable service quality is foundational to building long-term relationships with patients. By maintaining high standards of care and ensuring that patients consistently receive the same level of service, healthcare providers can foster loyalty and trust. Reliable service delivery encourages repeat visits, positive word-of-mouth, and long-term patient relationships. This consistency is key to value creation, contributing to a positive reputation and sustained growth for healthcare organizations.

24.4 Quick Check

1. From a patient's perspective, value in healthcare is primarily derived from which of the following?

a) The cost of treatment
b) Service quality, personalized care, and outcomes
c) The number of healthcare professionals employed
d) The technology used in healthcare facilities

2. From a provider's perspective, which of the following is most associated with creating value in healthcare?

a) Maximizing patient volume
b) Delivering high-quality care efficiently while maintaining financial sustainability
c) Offering the lowest prices
d) Limiting patient interactions to reduce costs

3. Which strategies focus on involving patients in their treatment plans and maintaining clear communication?

a) Value-based marketing
b) Patient-centred care and engagement
c) Preventive care and health management
d) Data-driven decision-making

4. What is the primary goal of value-based marketing in healthcare?

a) To promote healthcare services at the lowest price
b) To highlight benefits and outcomes that matter most to patients
c) To highlight new medical technologies
d) To emphasize operational efficiency

5. Which technological innovation is NOT typically associated with enhancing value in healthcare?

a) Telemedicine
b) Electronic health records
c) AI-driven diagnostics
d) Reducing patient waiting times through automation

6. What is the key benefit of focusing on preventive care and health management?

a) Reducing healthcare costs over time by preventing chronic conditions
b) Maximizing patient revenue through continuous treatments
c) Offering immediate treatment for patients with urgent health needs
d) Enhancing administrative efficiency

7. How does operational efficiency contribute to value creation in healthcare?

a) It leads to higher patient prices
b) It improves service delivery and reduces costs, benefiting patients and providers
c) It increases the number of healthcare providers available
d) It eliminates the need for staff training

8. Why is developing a skilled and engaged workforce essential for value creation in healthcare?

a) Skilled healthcare workers reduce the overall costs of healthcare services
b) Engaged staff are more likely to deliver high-quality care and build positive patient relationships
c) Skilled workers are less likely to require training
d) Staff engagement is irrelevant to patient satisfaction

9. Which of the following is a key benefit of building sustainable practices in healthcare?

a) Higher patient charges
b) Improved patient loyalty and satisfaction
c) Reduced focus on patient care quality
d) Increased staff turnover

10. What is the primary purpose of data-driven decision-making in healthcare marketing?

a) To reduce patient waiting times
b) To predict patient needs, personalize care, and optimize service delivery
c) To increase the cost of services offered
d) To minimize patient interaction

11. How does fostering long-term relationships with patients contribute to value creation?

a) It reduces the need for new marketing efforts
b) It leads to repeated visits, positive word-of-mouth, and sustained growth for healthcare organizations
c) It increases patient turnover
d) It encourages patients to seek cheaper alternatives

12. Consistent and reliable service quality in healthcare is key to:

a) Reducing the number of staff required
b) Enhancing patient satisfaction and building long-term relationships
c) Cutting operational costs significantly
d) Offering limited services to patients

Correct answers

1- b

2- b

3- b

4- b

5- d

6- a

7- b

8- b

9- b

10-b

11- b

12- b

24.5 Real-Life Case Study: Kaiser Permanente – Integrated Care Model for Value Creation

Case Overview

Kaiser Permanente, a leader in integrated healthcare, has excelled in creating value by merging care delivery with health insurance to provide seamless, patient-centered services. Their approach focuses on preventive care, technology integration, and operational efficiency to improve patient outcomes and satisfaction.

Key Strategies Implemented:

1. Integrated Care Model

Kaiser Permanente combines healthcare services and insurance under one roof, allowing for streamlined care coordination and reduced administrative burdens. Patients experience better continuity of care and fewer gaps in treatment plans.

2. Emphasis on Preventive Care

They launched wellness initiatives, including screenings, lifestyle coaching, and chronic disease management programs, to proactively address health issues before they escalate.

3. Technological Innovation

Kaiser Permanente's HealthConnect system is a comprehensive electronic health records (EHR) platform that enables providers and patients to access real-time medical histories, lab results, and prescriptions.

4. Patient Engagement

The organization encourages active patient participation through online portals and mobile apps, which offer appointment scheduling, virtual consultations, and health education resources.

Results:

- Improved patient satisfaction due to seamless service delivery.

- Reduced healthcare costs by focusing on prevention and early intervention.

- Increased operational efficiency, enabling high-quality care at scale.

Discussion Questions

1. Value Creation in Healthcare Marketing

- How does Kaiser Permanente's integrated care model enhance patient satisfaction and organizational efficiency?

2. Patient-Cantered Care and Engagement

- In what ways do Kaiser Permanente's preventive care and digital tools align with patient-centered value creation?

3. Sustainability and Long-Term Value

- How does integrating technology and preventive care contribute to long-term sustainability for Kaiser Permanente?

4. Data-Driven Decision-Making

- How can other healthcare providers leverage data analytics like Kaiser Permanente's Health Connect system to improve patient outcomes?

Chapter 25: Patient-Centric Marketing

25.1 Understanding Healthcare Consumers

• Decision-Making Process: In the healthcare sector, patient decisions are influenced by personal factors, external influences, and digital platforms. While some patients make independent decisions, many are guided by providers, family, or social media insights. Healthcare marketing must account for these varied influences to be effective.

• Role of Emotions and Trust: Trust is central to healthcare relationships. Patients are more likely to engage with providers they feel are transparent, ethical, and focused on their well-being. Emotions are significant in healthcare decisions, often guiding patients' interactions with services and professionals. Building strong emotional connections through empathy and trust is key to patient retention and satisfaction.

25.2 Applying the Golden Circle Method in Healthcare

Why "Why" Matters:
In healthcare marketing, the "Why" represents the core purpose of a healthcare provider's services, which extends beyond mere treatment or diagnosis. The "Why" focuses on improving patient outcomes, enhancing quality of life, and fostering long-term health benefits. It emphasizes why the provider does what they do— such as their commitment to holistic patient care, prevention, or personalized health management. By communicating this purpose clearly, healthcare organizations can create deeper emotional connections with patients, which builds trust and loyalty.

Focusing on the Bigger Picture:
The "Why" in healthcare doesn't just focus on curing illnesses or performing procedures; it also highlights the ongoing mission of enhancing patients' quality of life through every interaction. This

includes preventive care, health education, and continuous support to help patients manage chronic conditions. When a healthcare provider communicates its "Why" clearly, it inspires patients to feel involved in their care and invested in their health outcomes.

25.3 Tribal Marketing in Healthcare

Concept of Tribal Marketing:
Tribal marketing in healthcare is building patient communities around shared values, experiences, and common health goals. The concept stems from the idea that people often form emotional connections and loyalty with brands that reflect their personal beliefs or experiences. In healthcare, this means creating physical or digital spaces where patients feel they belong and can engage with others who share similar health concerns.

Tribal marketing can take shape in several ways, such as providing personalized care that reflects patients' values, creating support groups for specific conditions (like diabetes or cancer), or using digital platforms to keep patients informed and connected. This sense of community helps to nurture trust, loyalty, and engagement, as patients feel they are part of a tribe that supports their health journey.

The Role of Personalized Care in Tribal Marketing

At its core, tribal marketing in healthcare revolves around fostering a sense of belonging. This involves offering personalized care tailored to individual patient's needs and interests, making them feel valued as part of the healthcare organization's community. For example, a healthcare provider that offers personalized health tips, responds to patient feedback and creates spaces for open dialogue (like forums or social media groups) can strengthen the bond with their patients, encouraging loyalty and satisfaction.

By nurturing these patient communities, healthcare providers can go beyond transactional relationships and create long-term connections. This approach leverages the power of shared health journeys and mutual support, ensuring that patients feel part of something larger than their treatment, an interconnected network of care and support that fosters long-term engagement.

25.4 Understanding Patient Needs and Expectations

• Empathy and Active Listening: Patient-centric marketing requires healthcare providers to prioritize active listening. Understanding diverse patient needs—whether through digital communication or in-person consultations—enables the creation of tailored, empathetic responses that address individual concerns.

• Addressing Patient Pain Points: Common patient pain points such as accessibility, wait times, and the complexity of treatment options must be tackled directly. Healthcare marketing strategies should focus on solving these issues by offering accessible digital solutions, clear communication, and patient-friendly interfaces.

Enhancing Patient Experiences

• Effective Communication Strategies: Developing clear, empathetic, and reassuring communication techniques helps healthcare providers engage patients meaningfully. Digital tools and platforms should be leveraged to provide patients with real-time information, updates, and personalized messages that ensure clarity and comfort.

• Creating a Supportive Environment: Beyond just clinical care, healthcare settings should focus on comfort and personalization. Creating a supportive environment enhances patient satisfaction and retention, from digital touchpoints to in-clinic interactions. This may include user-friendly platforms, empathetic staff, and personalized care plans that cater to each patient's needs.

25.5 Retention and Loyalty Programs

• Follow-up and Engagement: Post-visit engagement strengthens ongoing relationships, mainly through digital platforms. Strengths include follow-up emails, health tips, or reminders about health management practices. Maintaining continuous engagement is key to long-term patient satisfaction and loyalty.

• Loyalty and Feedback Systems: Designing loyalty programs that reward patients for their engagement, such as personalized health resources, discounts on services, or exclusive content, can significantly enhance retention. Additionally, actively collecting feedback through surveys or digital tools can help healthcare providers refine services and respond to evolving patient needs.

25.6 Quick Check

1. What influences patient decision-making in the healthcare sector?

a) Only personal factors
b) Only external influences
c) A combination of personal factors, external influences, and digital platforms
d) Only digital platforms

2. What is central to building strong healthcare relationships with patients?

a) Offering the lowest price
b) Emotional connections, empathy, and trust
c) Minimizing patient-provider interactions
d) Focusing solely on treatment outcomes

3. In healthcare marketing, the "Why" refers to:

a) The specific treatments offered by the provider
b) The core purpose behind a provider's services, such as improving patient outcomes
c) The cost of healthcare services
d) The type of healthcare technology used

4. What does focus on the "Why" in healthcare marketing aim to inspire in patients?

a) An interest in trying new treatment methods
b) A sense of involvement in their care and investment in their health outcomes
c) A desire to explore a broader range of services
d) Increased focus on medical procedures

5. What is the concept of tribal marketing in healthcare?

a) Offering the lowest cost of treatment
b) Building patient communities around shared health goals and values
c) Relying solely on digital platforms for patient engagement
d) Focusing only on high-end patient services

6. How can personalized care enhance tribal marketing in healthcare?

a) By offering general care for all patients without tailoring it to individual needs
b) By fostering a sense of belonging through personalized care, health tips, and patient feedback
c) By reducing the time spent on each patient
d) By focusing exclusively on clinical outcomes

7. What is essential for patient-centric marketing?

a) Ignoring patient feedback
b) Prioritizing active listening and understanding diverse patient needs
c) Reducing the number of available healthcare options
d) Limiting communication with patients after treatment

8. Which of the following is a typical patient pain point that health-care marketing strategies should address?

a) High-quality treatment
b) Accessibility, wait times, and complexity of treatment options
c) Convenient payment methods
d) Number of healthcare professionals available

9. How can healthcare providers enhance patient experiences?

a) By reducing the number of interactions with patients
b) By focusing on clinical care only
c) By developing clear, empathetic communication and creating a supportive environment
d) By offering the cheapest services

10. What is the purpose of follow-up and engagement in patient retention?

a) To increase the number of patient visits
b) To strengthen ongoing relationships and maintain patient satisfaction through digital platforms
c) To reduce healthcare costs for patients
d) To limit patient contact to only necessary follow-ups

11. What roles do loyalty and feedback systems play in healthcare marketing?

a) They increase the frequency of patient visits
b) They reward patients for engagement and help providers refine services based on patient feedback
c) They focus solely on reducing the costs of services
d) They prioritize attracting new patients over retaining existing ones

Correct answers

1- c

2- b

3- b

4- b

5- b

6- b

7- b

8- b

9- c

10- b

11- b

25.7 Real-Life Case Study: Cleveland Clinic – Patient-Centric Marketing and Emotional Engagement

Case Overview Cleveland Clinic, a leading non-profit academic medical center, has embraced patient-centric marketing strategies that integrate emotional engagement, trust-building, and the concept of patient communities. Their approach focuses on providing clear, empathetic communication, leveraging digital tools, and fostering a sense of belonging among patients while addressing their core emotional and physical needs.

Key Strategies Implemented:

1. Emotional Engagement & Trust Building Cleveland Clinic's marketing strategy centers on trust, emphasizing the emotional connection between patients and healthcare providers. Their famous advertising campaign, "Empathy," used a powerful emotional narrative highlighting how doctors can build meaningful relationships with patients, focusing on empathy and compassion as the foundation of care. This campaign resonated with patients, helping to enhance trust and loyalty.

2. Tribal Marketing through Patient Communities Cleveland Clinic has developed strong online patient communities. For example, they have specialized groups for individuals with heart disease, cancer, and other chronic conditions. Through these groups, patients share their experiences and provide mutual support. Cleveland Clinic's digital platforms allow patients to connect with others who understand their health journey, fostering a sense of belonging.

3. Personalized Care and Patient Needs: The organization uses digital tools to create personalized care experiences. The Cleveland Clinic mobile app allows patients to manage appointments, access their health records, and communicate directly with healthcare providers. This personalizes the patient experience, making patients feel more involved in their care and enhancing their sense of ownership over their health.

4. Focus on Empathy and Active Listening: Cleveland Clinic's care model emphasizes active listening and empathy. Healthcare providers are trained to truly listen to patient concerns, which helps to craft individualized treatment plans. This approach builds patient trust and addresses common pain points like communication gaps or a lack of personalized care.

Results:

• Increased Patient Satisfaction: Emotional engagement and clear communication led to higher patient satisfaction rates and loyalty.

• Stronger Patient Retention: Cleveland Clinic maintained strong relationships with patients through loyalty programs and follow-up engagement, improving retention and long-term engagement.

• Enhanced Community and Trust: Cleveland Clinic built an intense sense of belonging among its patients by creating online communities and offering continuous support, strengthening brand loyalty and trust.

Discussion Questions

1. Role of Emotions and Trust in Healthcare Marketing

• How did Cleveland Clinic use emotional marketing and trust-building strategies to enhance patient loyalty and satisfaction?

2. Tribal Marketing in Healthcare

• In what ways did Cleveland Clinic implement tribal marketing to foster patient communities, and what impact did this have on patient engagement?

3. Understanding Patient Needs and Expectations

• How did Cleveland Clinic prioritize patient needs through personalized care, and how does this approach improve patient experiences?

4. Empathy and Active Listening

• How does Cleveland Clinic's emphasis on empathy and active listening influence patient retention, and how could other healthcare providers replicate this in their marketing strategies?

5. Retention and Loyalty Programs

• What specific follow-up and engagement strategies did Cleveland Clinic use to retain patients, and how did these strategies contribute to the organization's success in patient retention?

Chapter 26: Building the Healthcare Brand

26.1 Brand Identity in Healthcare

• Elements of a Trusted Healthcare Brand:

A trusted healthcare brand conveys quality, compassion, and reliability. Essential elements include a clear mission, consistent visual identity (logo, color schemes, and typography), and adherence to high ethical and medical standards. For example, the Mayo Clinic's brand emphasizes expert care and innovation while maintaining a patient-centric focus, making it one of the most trusted names in healthcare.

• Building a Brand That Resonates with Patients:

A thriving healthcare brand creates emotional connections by addressing patient needs and concerns. Personalization plays a crucial role. For instance, Cleveland Clinic incorporates patient stories in its marketing to highlight its commitment to delivering care with empathy. Understanding cultural nuances and addressing regional health challenges also helps resonate with diverse patient demographics.

Communicating the Brand Effectively

- Crafting Key Messages That Reflect Values and Expertise:
Effective branding highlights an organization's core values, such
as compassion, excellence, and expertise in specialized fields. For
example, a children's hospital may focus its messaging on creating
a safe and joyful healing environment for young patients.

- Engaging Patients Through Storytelling:
Storytelling humanizes a healthcare brand, making it relatable and
memorable. Sharing patient recovery stories, like overcoming
critical illnesses through advanced treatments, can inspire and
reassure potential patients. For instance, campaigns by Johns
Hopkins share in-depth patient journeys to emphasize the hospital's
innovative therapies and compassionate care.

26.2 Reputation Management

- **Handling Patient Reviews and Feedback:**
Online reviews significantly impact a healthcare organization's
reputation. Actively responding to both positive and negative
reviews fosters trust. For example, addressing a negative review
with a message like, "We're sorry to hear about your experience.
Please contact us to resolve the issue," demonstrates accountability
and willingness to improve.

- **Maintaining Trust and Credibility:**
Transparency in operations, such as sharing performance metrics
and certifications, enhances credibility. Hospitals like Kaiser
Permanente publicly share quality metrics and patient safety
initiatives, building trust among patients and stakeholders.

26.3 Branding and Emotional Connections

- **Healthcare Branding: Developing Emotionally Based Consumer-Brand Relationships:**

Patients often choose healthcare providers based on emotional factors such as trust, comfort, and hope. For instance, St. Jude Children's Research Hospital focuses on emotional appeals in its branding, highlighting its commitment to curing childhood cancer at no cost to families.

- **How to Create Strong Emotional Connections with Patients:**

To strengthen emotional ties, use personalized care, regular engagement through follow-up calls, and empathy-driven messaging. For example, post-treatment check-ins or sending health tips via email can make patients feel valued beyond their appointments.

26.4 Quick Check

1. What is an essential element of a trusted healthcare brand?

a) A catchy slogan
b) A clear mission, consistent visual identity, and adherence to
ethical standards
c) Low-cost healthcare services
d) Expensive marketing campaigns

2. How does Cleveland Clinic resonate with patients in its branding?

a) By focusing solely on medical treatments
b) By incorporating patient stories into their marketing to highlight
empathy
c) By offering the lowest cost of care
d) By minimizing patient interactions

3. What is the primary role of storytelling in healthcare branding?

a) To focus on technical jargon and procedures
b) To humanize the brand and make it relatable by sharing patient
recovery stories
c) To reduce the need for patient engagement
d) To emphasize financial success

4. How should healthcare providers handle patient reviews and
feedback?

a) Ignore negative reviews
b) Actively respond to both positive and negative reviews to foster
trust
c) Remove all negative feedback from online platforms
d) Focus only on positive reviews

5. What is an effective method for creating emotional connections with patients?

a) Offering discounts on treatments
b) Regular engagement through follow-up calls and personalized health messages
c) Reducing patient interaction after treatment
d) Limiting communication to in-clinic visits

6. What is a key aspect of HIPAA-compliant social media use?

a) Sharing patient information freely for promotional purposes
b) Avoiding the use of patient data without explicit consent
c) Sharing identifiable patient data with consent
d) Using social media for only internal purposes

Correct answers:

1- b

2- b

3- b

4- b

5- b

6- b

26.5 Case Study: St. Jude Children's Research Hospital – Building an Emotionally Driven Healthcare Brand

St. Jude Children's Research Hospital has established itself as one of the most emotionally resonant healthcare brands by focusing on its core mission: to treat and defeat childhood cancer. What sets St. Jude apart is its strong, compassionate, and mission-driven brand identity, which communicates hope, resilience, and care to both patients and their families. The hospital's brand emphasizes its commitment to providing care without charge to families, which resonates deeply with donors, patients, and the public.

St. Jude's brand is built around its emotional appeal, with patient stories at the heart of its messaging. These stories highlight the hospital's life-saving treatments and reinforce the institution's commitment to giving children a chance at life, regardless of their financial background. The hospital uses various storytelling methods, from written testimonials to video documentaries, to ensure its message is both heartfelt and impactful.

The hospital's visual identity plays a pivotal role in reinforcing its brand. The St. Jude logo, which incorporates an image of a child, is instantly recognizable and conveys the organization's focus on pediatric care. The consistent use of red, white, and dark gray in their branding creates a sense of urgency, warmth, and compassion, essential qualities for a healthcare brand that deals with sensitive issues like childhood illness.

Moreover, the hospital maintains transparency in its operations, making financial and operational details accessible to the public. This transparency builds trust, particularly with donors who feel confident that their contributions directly impact the hospital's work. St. Jude also engages patients and their families by providing continuous emotional support through follow-up calls, newsletters, and unique events, ensuring patients feel valued long after their treatment ends.

St. Jude Children's Research Hospital has become synonymous with hope, care, and compassionate treatment through its emotionally driven branding efforts. Its brand effectively connects with local and global audiences, making it a prime example of how a healthcare organization can use emotional connections to build trust and loyalty.

Discussion Questions:

1. Elements of a Trusted Healthcare Brand:

• What elements of St. Jude's brand identity contribute to its trustworthiness? How do these elements align with the hospital's mission to provide free care to children with cancer?

2. Building a Brand that Resonates with Patients:

• In what ways does St. Jude's storytelling approach create emotional connections with its audience? How does incorporating patient stories into marketing materials help build trust and loyalty?

3. Crafting Key Messages that Reflect Values and Expertise:

• How does St. Jude communicate its core values of compassion, hope, and excellence in care through its marketing materials and patient stories? How do these messages reinforce its position as a leader in pediatric healthcare?

4. Engaging Patients Through Storytelling:

• How does using personal patient stories make St. Jude's brand more relatable and memorable? How can other healthcare providers use similar storytelling techniques to enhance their branding?

5. Reputation Management:

• How does St. Jude manage its reputation through transparency, especially regarding financial and operational openness? What role does transparency play in strengthening public trust?

6. Branding and Emotional Connections:

• How does St. Jude's emotional branding strategy influence the decision-making process of donors and potential patients? How important is it for healthcare brands to foster emotional ties with their audience?

7. Consistency in Visual Identity:

• How does St. Jude's use of visual elements (like its logo and color scheme) contribute to a cohesive brand experience? How do these visual cues help strengthen the hospital's emotional appeal to its audience?

Chapter 27: Digital Marketing in Healthcare

27.1 Social Media in Healthcare

Using Social Platforms for Patient Education: social media has revolutionized healthcare education, providing a direct and engaging way to inform and connect with patients.

Sharing Educational Content

o Platforms like Facebook, Instagram, and LinkedIn enable healthcare providers to disseminate helpful information, such as disease prevention tips, vaccination benefits, and healthy lifestyle advice.

o Infographics and videos simplify complex medical topics, making them accessible to a broad audience.

Hosting Interactive Sessions

• Live Q&A sessions on platforms like Facebook and Instagram allow patients to engage directly with healthcare professionals, ask questions, and gain real-time insights.

• These sessions build trust and help demystify medical procedures or treatments.

Showcasing Success Stories and Updates

• Sharing patient success stories or updates on medical advancements fosters credibility and strengthens the provider-patient relationship.

• Example: The Cleveland Clinic's Twitter account frequently shares practical health tips and medical breakthroughs, making it a valuable patient resource.

Targeting Specific Audiences

Tailor content to meet the needs of demographics. For instance:

• Maternity clinics can share prenatal care tips or host Facebook groups for expectant mothers.

• Paediatricians can use TikTok to create engaging videos for parents on children's health.

Humanizing Healthcare

• Use Instagram Stories or short video clips to highlight the daily lives of healthcare staff, highlighting their dedication and expertise.

• Behind-the-scenes content helps patients connect emotionally with the organization.

Encouraging Community Engagement

• Create opportunities for patients to participate in discussions or share their experiences.

• Polls, surveys, and challenges can foster interaction and make healthcare discussions more relatable.

Guidelines for HIPAA-Compliant Social Media Use: Ensuring patient privacy is critical. Avoid sharing identifiable patient information without explicit consent. An example of compliance would be using anonymized patient data when discussing treatment successes online.

27.2 Healthcare Content Marketing

• Writing Blogs, Newsletters, and Educational Content:
Regularly publishing health-related content positions an organization as an authority. For example, a blog about managing diabetes can include actionable tips, expert interviews, and patient testimonials to engage readers.

• Developing a Patient-Focused Content Calendar:
Content planning ensures the timely delivery of relevant topics. For instance, during flu season, hospitals can schedule posts about vaccination drives and preventive measures, while Heart Health Month can be an opportunity to share cardiovascular care tips.

27.3 SEO and Website Best Practices

• Optimizing for Patient Queries and Local Searches:
Use keywords like "best cardiologist near me" or "emergency care in [city name]" to improve search rankings. Hospitals can also register on Google My Business to enhance local visibility.

- Creating User-Friendly and Accessible Websites:
Websites should be intuitive, with straightforward navigation and accessibility features like screen readers and multilingual support. Mount Sinai's website prioritizes patient needs with easy appointment scheduling and multilingual options.

27.4 The Mayo Clinic – Improving SEO

The Mayo Clinic, a globally recognized healthcare institution, has a diverse audience of patients worldwide. The clinic launched a blog highlighting stories from patients, families, and Mayo Clinic staff to connect these varied communities and boost its online presence. This initiative has become one of the most compelling examples of healthcare marketing, particularly in SEO.

The blog quickly became a valuable resource for patients with complex conditions. Its success in SEO is evident, as Mayo Clinic focused on publishing high-quality articles from the start. Healthcare experts, including Ph.D. holders like Joel Streed, write these pieces, which adds significant authority to their content.

Having specialists on board has also aided Mayo Clinic's link-building efforts. Major publications like the Seattle Times and Science began inviting Mayo Clinic writers to share their insights on public health issues. This exposure further cemented the Mayo Clinic's reputation as a leading authority in healthcare.

- How can healthcare institutions like the Mayo Clinic utilize blogs to educate diverse patient populations about complex conditions, and what makes the content of these blogs valuable to patients seeking information?

• In what ways can other healthcare providers replicate Mayo Clinic's strategy of publishing high-quality, expert-written articles to boost their SEO and attract a larger audience?

• How did Mayo Clinic's use of healthcare experts, such as Ph.D. holders, enhance the credibility of their blog content and contribute to their SEO success?

• How can healthcare providers integrate expert voices into their digital marketing efforts to establish themselves as trusted sources of information in their field?

• How can healthcare organizations tailor their digital content to engage specific patient demographics, such as creating condition-specific articles or addressing diverse health concerns through personalized blog posts?

• What role does creating content that resonates with various patient communities (e.g., for rare diseases and chronic conditions) play in increasing SEO performance and patient engagement?

• How does Mayo Clinic's commitment to publishing high-quality, authoritative content exemplify best practices in SEO for healthcare organizations?

• What key SEO techniques (e.g., keyword research, on-page optimization) should healthcare organizations consider when building a blog or content platform to improve their search rankings and online visibility?

27.5 Quick Check

1. What is the purpose of using social media in healthcare marketing?

a) To only promote healthcare services
b) To share educational content, host Q&A sessions, and engage with patients
c) To only post advertisements for medical equipment
d) To avoid patient interaction

2. How can healthcare providers humanize their brand on social media?

a) Post-technical medical procedures only
b) Share behind-the-scenes content highlighting the daily lives of healthcare staff
c) Focus solely on patient testimonials
d) Avoid showing any personal aspects of healthcare professionals

3. How can healthcare organizations optimize their website for local searches?

a) Using general terms like "best doctor."
b) Using local-specific keywords like "cardiologist near me" and registering on Google My Business
c) Focusing only on national searches
d) Ignoring search engine optimization entirely

4. How can healthcare providers engage with their audiences on social media?

a) By focusing only on advertisements
b) By hosting interactive sessions like live Q&As to address patient queries
c) By avoiding comments or patient interactions
d) By posting only one-way communication

5. What is the best practice for creating a user-friendly healthcare website?

a) Overloading the site with excessive information
b) Ensuring straightforward navigation, accessibility features, and multilingual support
c) Avoiding any interactive features
d) Limiting content to only emergency services

6. What is the benefit of using infographics and videos on social media for healthcare marketing?

a) They complicate the information
b) They make complex medical topics easier to understand and accessible to a broader audience
c) They only attract a specific age group
d) They focus on advertisements and sales

Correct answers

1- b

2- b

3- b

4- b

5- b

6- b

Chapter 28: Ethical and Regulatory Considerations in Healthcare Marketing

28.1 Ethical Considerations in Healthcare Marketing

- **Marketing Communications and Ethical Dilemmas:**
Ethical issues, such as exaggerating treatment outcomes, can significantly undermine patient trust and tarnish a healthcare provider's reputation. To maintain credibility, marketing efforts should prioritize honesty and transparency, relying on accurate data to support claims. For example, if promoting "high success rates," include verified statistics and clear disclaimers to ensure patients have realistic expectations.

- Overpromising services can lead to patient dissatisfaction when expectations are not met. Therefore, it is crucial only to promise what can be consistently delivered. Focus on exceeding expectations through exceptional service during the patient experience but ensure that the foundational promise is fulfilled to secure trust and satisfaction. This balanced approach fosters patient loyalty and enhances the provider's reputation.

- **Balancing Profit with Patient Well-Being:**
Strive for campaigns that prioritize health outcomes. For example, highlight affordable, preventive screenings instead of promoting expensive tests to ensure broader access.

- **Case Studies on Ethical Issues in Healthcare Marketing:**
Learn from examples like misleading weight-loss clinic ads, where claims were not scientifically validated. Ethical marketing avoids such pitfalls by adhering to the AMA Code of Medical Ethics guidelines.

28.2 Accrediting Bodies and Independent Verification

- The Role of Third-Party Organizations in Ensuring Quality and Trust:
Partnerships with accreditation bodies like Joint Commission International (JCI) assure patients of quality standards.

- How Hospitals Can Collaborate with Accrediting Bodies:
Displaying accreditation logos on websites and promotional materials builds credibility and confidence.

28.3 Ethics in Patient Communication

Ensuring Transparency and Trust in Messaging

Transparency is essential in healthcare marketing to build trust and empower patients. For instance, a weight-loss surgery campaign should highlight benefits and potential recovery challenges, ensuring realistic expectations. Communicating costs, timelines, and outcomes fosters confidence and reduces misunderstandings. Authentic testimonials and balanced case studies further reinforce trust.

Avoiding Manipulative or Misleading Tactics

Avoid fear-based marketing and sensationalized claims like "miracle cures," as they damage credibility. Instead, focus on empowering patients with accurate, evidence-based information. For example, a heart health campaign can emphasize proactive steps and personalized care options rather than alarming statistics. Ethical, honest messaging strengthens patient relationships and enhances long-term trust.

1. What is the primary ethical issue when exaggerating treatment outcomes in healthcare marketing?

a) It boosts patient confidence
b) It undermines patient trust and tarnishes the healthcare provider's reputation
c) It leads to higher patient satisfaction
d) It encourages more patients to visit the facility

2. What should healthcare providers do to avoid overpromising in their marketing communications?

a) Promise as much as possible to attract more patients
b) Focus on delivering what can be consistently achieved while exceeding expectations through exceptional service
c) Make unrealistic claims to outdo competitors
d) Only emphasize the positive aspects of treatment and ignore potential drawbacks

3. Why is it essential for healthcare marketing campaigns to balance profit with patient well-being?

a) To attract more investors
b) To focus on campaigns that prioritize health outcomes and ensure broader access to healthcare services
c) To make services appear more expensive and exclusive
d) To highlight only the high-end services and products

4. What is the role of accreditation bodies like the Joint Commission International (JCI) in healthcare marketing?

a) To regulate prices of healthcare services
b) To ensure quality standards and build patient trust
c) To manage hospital staff salaries
d) To provide marketing slogans for healthcare organizations

5. How can hospitals enhance their credibility by collaborating with accrediting bodies?

a) By displaying accreditation logos on websites and promotional materials
b) By hiding accreditation details to focus on their internal reputation
c) By avoiding any external verification of their services
d) By promoting unverified patient testimonials

6. What is an essential practice for ensuring transparency and trust in healthcare messaging?

a) Highlighting only the positive aspects of treatments without addressing potential risks
b) Providing honest, balanced communication about the benefits and challenges of treatments, including precise costs and outcomes
c) Using fear-based tactics to emphasize urgency and attract attention
d) Avoiding patient feedback and focusing on expert opinions

7. What marketing approach should be avoided to maintain ethical standards in healthcare marketing?

a) Empowering patients with accurate, evidence-based information
b) Providing testimonials from actual patients
c) Using fear-based marketing or sensationalized claims like "miracle cures."
d) Highlighting preventive health options and evidence-backed practices

Correct answers

1- b

2- b

3- b

4- b

5- a

6- b

7- c

28.5 Weight-Loss Clinics and Ethical Issues in Healthcare Marketing

A prominent case highlighting ethical issues in healthcare marketing involves misleading advertisements from weight-loss clinics. Several clinics made exaggerated claims about their treatments' effectiveness, promoting "miracle" weight-loss solutions without scientific backing. These clinics promised quick, dramatic results, often neglecting to communicate the treatments' risks or potential side effects.

For example, one clinic claimed their weight-loss program could help patients lose 20-30 pounds in weeks with minimal effort. However, after patients enrolled, many found that the results were either minimal or unsustainable. The clinics failed to meet their promises, leading to patient dissatisfaction, reputational damage, and legal action. These claims were later found unsupported by scientific evidence, and the clinics were forced to retract their advertising and offer refunds to patients. This case exemplifies how overpromising and unethical marketing practices can lead to loss of trust, legal consequences, and long-term damage to a brand's reputation.

Discussion Questions

1. Marketing Communications and Ethical Dilemmas:

• In what ways could the weight-loss clinic have marketed its services more ethically, ensuring transparency and patient trust?

• How can healthcare providers ensure that verifiable data back their marketing claims, and what steps can they take to avoid exaggerating treatment outcomes?

2. Overpromising Services:

• How can healthcare organizations balance promoting their services effectively without overpromising or setting unrealistic expectations for patients?

• What are the potential consequences of overpromising services, and how can healthcare providers recover from such mistakes?

3. Balancing Profit with Patient Well-Being:

• How can healthcare providers prioritize patient well-being while ensuring profitability in their marketing campaigns?

• Should healthcare providers focus more on affordable options like preventive screenings, even if they bring in less revenue than expensive treatments?

4. Ethics in Patient Communication:

• How can healthcare providers ensure transparency and clear communication in their marketing materials, especially regarding treatment risks and expected outcomes?

• Why is it essential to avoid fear-based marketing tactics, and what are some ethical alternatives for promoting patient care services?

Chapter 29: Charity Marketing and the Importance of Donations in Healthcare

29.1 Introduction to Charity Marketing in Healthcare

Charity marketing strategically promotes nonprofit causes to garner public support and financial donations. According to research by Fillis and Michael (2021) in "Charity Marketing: Contemporary Issues, Research, and Practice," traditional marketing tools combined with an emphasis on emotional engagement and transparency drive donor commitment. In healthcare, donations fund essential equipment, treatments, and research. For instance, campaigns highlighting the impact of advanced diagnostic machines in rural areas often garner significant public support.

29.2 Leveraging Storytelling and Emotional Appeal

Storytelling lies at the heart of successful charity marketing. Narratives about how donor contributions lead to life-changing healthcare outcomes can inspire generosity. For example, sharing the story of a child receiving life-saving surgery because of donor support creates an emotional resonance that motivates contributions. This aligns with Fillis and Michael's emphasis on the transformative power of personal stories in engaging stakeholders.

29.3 Celebrity Endorsements in Charity Marketing

Celebrities often amplify the outreach of healthcare charities. For instance, Angelina Jolie's advocacy for cancer awareness draws attention to research funding. However, Fillis and Michael highlight the importance of ensuring alignment between the celebrity's values and the charity's mission to maintain authenticity and trust.

29.4 Digital Transformation in Charity Marketing

Modern charity marketing integrates digital platforms for enhanced engagement. Social media campaigns, email newsletters, and interactive donor portals have become essential for reaching broader audiences. As Fillis and Michael suggest, these platforms provide avenues for sharing real-time updates, hosting virtual fundraisers, and offering transparent financial breakdowns.

29.5 Quick Check

1. What is the primary goal of charity marketing in healthcare?

a) To increase profits for healthcare providers
b) To garner public support and financial donations for healthcare causes
c) To promote commercial healthcare products
d) To reduce the cost of medical services

2. What roles do compelling patient recovery stories play in healthcare charity marketing?

a) They help reduce the cost of healthcare treatments
b) They educate donors on how funds are used and create an emotional connection, fostering recurring contributions
c) They increase the number of healthcare professionals employed
d) They focus on advertising paid healthcare services

3. How does storytelling contribute to successful charity marketing in healthcare?

a) It creates financial instability for healthcare organizations
b) It builds emotional resonance by showcasing the impact of donations on life-changing healthcare outcomes
c) It distracts from the actual needs of the healthcare sector
d) It primarily promotes healthcare services and products

4. Why is celebrity endorsement important in healthcare charity marketing?

a) It ensures a significant increase in healthcare product sales
b) It amplifies the outreach of healthcare charities, drawing attention to the causes they support
c) It provides funding for healthcare campaigns without the need for public donations
d) It replaces the need for transparency in fundraising efforts

5. According to Fillis and Michael, What is a key element of modern charity marketing in healthcare?

a) Focusing solely on traditional print media campaigns
b) Integrating digital platforms such as social media, email newsletters, and interactive donor portals for enhanced engagement
c) Limiting outreach to local communities
d) Relying exclusively on in-person events for fundraising

6. What is the benefit of transparent financial breakdowns in healthcare charity marketing?

a) It discourages potential donors
b) It provides donors with real-time updates and builds trust in the charity's financial integrity
c) It limits the reach of the campaign
d) It makes the campaign less interactive and less engaging

Correct answers

1- b

2- b

3- b

4- b

5- b

6- b

29.6 Case: Carilion Clinic

Carilion Clinic in Virginia launched a breast cancer awareness campaign on the social media platform X, using the hashtag #YESMAMM. As part of the campaign, they encouraged followers to post their questions about breast cancer, which the clinic addressed online. With early detection being a critical factor in breast cancer treatment, the campaign emphasized the importance of scheduling screenings at Carilion's clinics. This raised awareness and drove organic traffic to their website, resulting in increased appointments. The hashtag #YESMAMM continues to be widely associated with breast cancer awareness, significantly boosting Carilion Clinic's visibility and positive recognition. This successful initiative is regarded as one of the best examples of healthcare marketing on social media.

Discussion Questions:

How did Carilion Clinic effectively use the social media platform X to promote breast cancer awareness through the hashtag #YESMAMM, and what aspects of this campaign contributed to its success?

In what ways did the campaign drive both awareness and action (increased website traffic and appointments), and how can other healthcare organizations replicate this success?

How does Carilion Clinic's approach to encouraging followers to ask questions about breast cancer reflect the emotional engagement that is central to charity marketing in healthcare?

How can healthcare providers incorporate storytelling into their marketing campaigns to create an emotional connection with their audience and inspire further engagement or donations?

Chapter 30: Public Healthcare Marketing - Challenges and PR Solutions

30.1 Challenges in Public Healthcare Systems

- Resource Limitations and Access Issues:

Public healthcare systems often struggle with resource constraints such as staffing shortages, outdated equipment, or limited funding. For example, rural hospitals may lack access to advanced diagnostic tools, creating disparities in care. Marketing can highlight these challenges while seeking public or private support.

- Balancing Demand with Capacity:

Public hospitals often face overcrowding. Marketing campaigns can educate patients about alternative care options, such as telemedicine or local clinics, reducing the burden on central hospitals.

30.2 Role of Healthcare Marketing in Raising Awareness

- Disease Prevention Campaigns:

Effective marketing can promote vaccination drives or screenings. For example, India's "Pulse Polio" campaign successfully eradicated polio through widespread awareness and free vaccination programs.

- Educating the Public on Treatment Options:

Campaigns can clarify treatment availability, such as accessible mental health services. For instance, the UK's NHS extensively promoted its mental health helpline during the COVID-19 pandemic.

30.3 Role of PR in Improving Public Healthcare Perceptions

• Building Positive Narratives:
PR strategies can highlight success stories, such as patients recovering from critical illnesses due to innovative treatments. For example, displaying a patient's recovery journey through a liver transplant funded by a government scheme can build trust in public healthcare systems.

• Crisis Management:
Clear and transparent communication fosters public trust during a crisis like a disease outbreak. Singapore's Ministry of Health effectively used regular press releases during the SARS outbreak to manage public concerns.

30.4 Case Studies on Successful Public Healthcare PR Campaigns

• The "Safe Hands" Campaign by WHO:
This initiative educated millions on proper handwashing techniques to curb the spread of infectious diseases. Social media challenges and influencer participation amplified its reach globally.

• South Africa's HIV/AIDS Awareness Campaigns:
These campaigns combined mass media with grassroots efforts, leading to a significant increase in testing and treatment.

Communicating Public Healthcare Improvements and Success Stories

• Sharing before-and-after metrics, such as improved survival rates after introducing advanced equipment, builds credibility. For instance, a hospital might publish statistics showing a 20% decrease in infant mortality after acquiring neonatal intensive care units.

30.5 Quick Check 

1. What is one of the primary challenges in public healthcare systems?

a) Overabundance of resources
b) Resource limitations and access issues, such as staffing shortages and outdated equipment
c) Excessive funding
d) Lack of patient interest in healthcare services

2. How can healthcare marketing help balance the demand with capacity in public hospitals?

a) By encouraging patients to visit hospitals more frequently
b) By educating patients about alternative care options, such as telemedicine or local clinics
c) By reducing the number of patients receiving care
d) By increasing the number of staff in hospitals

3. How can disease prevention campaigns contribute to public health?

a) By limiting public awareness of vaccination drives or screenings
b) By promoting vaccination drives and screenings to reduce the spread of diseases
c) By discouraging people from seeking healthcare services
d) By focusing only on expensive treatments

4. What is the key role of public relations (PR) in improving public healthcare perceptions?

a) Generating profits for public hospitals
b) Building positive narratives through success stories and innovative treatments
c) Focusing on negative aspects of healthcare to reduce public expectations
d) Limiting communication during a health crisis

5. How did Singapore manage public concerns during the SARS outbreak?

a) By minimizing communication with the public
b) By using regular press releases to provide clear and transparent communication
c) By focusing only on private healthcare systems
d) By delaying public announcements to avoid panic

6. What impact did the "Safe Hands" campaign by WHO have on public health?

a) It raised awareness about proper handwashing techniques to curb the spread of infectious diseases
b) It increased hospital admissions significantly
c) It discouraged vaccination practices
d) It focused solely on promoting expensive treatments

7. How can sharing before-and-after metrics, such as improved survival rates, benefit public healthcare?

a) It decreases public trust in healthcare systems
b) It builds credibility by displaying the impact of improvements, such as advanced equipment
c) It leads to an increased burden on healthcare staff
d) It reduces the number of patients seeking care

Correct answers

1- b

2- b

3- b

4- b

5- b

6- a

7- b

30.6 Arkansas Children's Hospital – Develop an Awareness Campaign

Arkansas Children's Hospital discovered that the risk of death for children and teens is significantly higher between Memorial Day and Labor Day. In response, the hospital launched an awareness campaign using the hashtag #100DeadliestDays to highlight this alarming statistic. The shocking nature of this information made it easily shareable, making it perfect for social media marketing. The hospital also invited local organizations, including police and road safety groups, to join the campaign, sharing tips on preventing road accidents and spreading the message. This collaborative approach amplified the campaign's reach and effectiveness in promoting safety.

Questions

How does the #100DeadliestDays campaign help raise awareness about public health risks during resource-constrained periods (e.g., summer)? Can similar campaigns address resource limitations in public healthcare systems, like staffing or equipment shortages?

What role can public healthcare marketing play in seeking public and private support to address these limitations?

In the context of Arkansas Children's Hospital's campaign, how could promoting alternative solutions (such as emergency care or preventive programs) alleviate the pressure on hospital emergency rooms during peak times like the summer?

How can public healthcare marketing help educate the public about the capacity challenges healthcare systems face, mainly when high demand exists?

Chapter 31: Challenges and Future Trends in Healthcare Marketing

31.1 Challenges in Healthcare Marketing

Regulatory Limitations and Patient Skepticism: Healthcare marketing must adhere to strict regulations to avoid misleading claims about treatments and outcomes. For instance, the FDA regulates how pharmaceutical products can be advertised to ensure they are not exaggerated. Transparency is key to overcoming skepticism. Providing clear, evidence-based information and using patient testimonials or peer-reviewed studies can help build trust. Ensuring patients understand treatments' benefits and risks fosters informed decision-making and reduces mistrust.

Addressing Disparities in Healthcare Access: Healthcare marketing must also focus on bridging the gap in access, especially for underserved populations. Mobile clinics and telehealth services effectively deliver care in remote areas. Campaigns promoting these services help ensure inclusiveness, especially for populations that may not have easy access to healthcare. Highlighting the success stories of patients who have benefited from these services can encourage engagement and foster trust.

31.2 Future Trends in Healthcare Marketing

• The Role of Digital Transformation in Healthcare Marketing

Digital innovations like AI-powered chatbots, telemedicine platforms, and wearable health devices are increasingly shaping the healthcare industry. These technologies enhance convenience, accessibility, and patient outcomes, but their marketing requires careful messaging around their practical benefits and safety. For example, Apple's marketing for its health-monitoring features in the Apple Watch highlights how the device can track essential health metrics like heart rate and ECG while ensuring user privacy and reliability (Apple, 2020). Demonstrating these technologies' real-world applications and evidence-based results is crucial to gaining patient trust and increasing adoption.

- The Impact of Emerging Technologies Like AR/VR in Healthcare
Augmented Reality (AR) and Virtual Reality (VR) are emerging as powerful patient education and engagement tools. VR, for instance, can simulate surgical procedures, allowing patients to understand what to expect and reducing anxiety (Kato, 2021). Marketing campaigns focusing on VR applications can highlight immersive tools such as virtual pain management or mental health therapies, showcasing how these technologies make healthcare experiences more interactive and less intimidating for tech-savvy patients. Demonstrating actual patient outcomes or testimonials from those who have benefited from these tools can also strengthen credibility.

31.3 Marketing Strategies for the Next Decade

As healthcare marketing continues to evolve, the following strategies are set to play a critical role in enhancing patient engagement and care:

1- Hyper-Personalization in Healthcare Marketing

Hyper-personalization tailors marketing efforts to individual patient needs based on their behaviors and preferences. By leveraging data from wearables and health apps, healthcare providers can send customized recommendations. For example, personalized reminders for medication and health habits can improve patient engagement.

2- Predictive Analytics for Proactive Care

Predictive analytics use patient data to forecast health risks, offering providers proactive care. Healthcare marketers can target at-risk patients by analyzing trends with tailored prevention messages or intervention tips, making care more anticipatory and personalized (Nnamdi, 2024).

3- Integration of Healthcare Services with Everyday Devices

Integrating healthcare into everyday devices like smartphones and wearables enables continuous health monitoring. Apps linked to smartwatches can track heart rate, activity, and sleep patterns, encouraging ongoing health management and keeping patients engaged in their care.

31.3 Quick Check 

1. What is one of the challenges in healthcare marketing related to regulatory limitations?

a) Misleading claims about treatments and outcomes
b) Lack of patient testimonials
c) Over-promoting mobile clinics
d) Providing too much evidence-based information

2. How can healthcare marketing overcome patient skepticism?

a) By avoiding evidence-based information
b) By using exaggerated treatment claims
c) By providing clear, evidence-based information and using patient testimonials
d) By focusing only on promoting high-cost treatments

3. What is one-way healthcare marketing can address disparities in healthcare access?

a) By limiting campaigns to urban populations
b) By focusing on high-income areas only
c) By promoting mobile clinics and telehealth services for underserved populations
d) By ignoring the needs of underserved populations

4. How does digital transformation influence healthcare marketing?

a) By focusing solely on traditional marketing methods
b) By introducing AI-powered chatbots, telemedicine platforms, and wearable health devices
c) By reducing patient engagement
d) By eliminating the need for evidence-based results

5. What is one potential use of Augmented Reality (AR) and Virtual Reality (VR) in healthcare marketing?

a) Limiting patient education
b) Simulating surgical procedures to reduce patient anxiety
c) Reducing the need for patient engagement
d) Eliminating real-world applications and patient outcomes

6. What is hyper-personalization in healthcare marketing?

a) Tailoring marketing efforts based on general patient needs
b) Focusing only on large groups of patients
c) Customizing marketing based on individual patient behaviors and preferences
d) Ignoring patient data for marketing purposes

7. How does predictive analytics enhance healthcare marketing?

a) By offering generic messages to all patients
b) By forecasting health risks and providing proactive care recommendations
c) By reducing the use of data in marketing strategies
d) By ignoring individual patient data

8. How does integrating healthcare services with everyday devices benefit patients?

a) By discouraging continuous health monitoring
b) By providing ongoing health management through smartphones and wearables
c) By focusing only on in-person appointments
d) By limiting the use of smart devices in healthcare

Correct answers

1- a

2- c

3- c

4- b

5- b

6- c

7- b

8- b

31.4 Real-Life Case: CVS Health – Reducing Disparities in Healthcare Access

Case Overview: CVS Health, a prominent healthcare provider, launched several initiatives to reduce healthcare disparities and improve access for underserved populations. One such initiative is their partnership with MinuteClinic and promoting telehealth services. The company focused on providing convenient access to healthcare through mobile clinics and telemedicine, especially in rural or low-income urban areas. By offering services such as flu shots, health screenings, and remote consultations via telehealth, CVS Health targeted populations that traditionally face barriers to healthcare access.

In its marketing campaign, CVS emphasized the affordability and convenience of these services. It also used success stories of individuals who benefited from these services to build trust and increase engagement. Through social media, email campaigns, and partnerships with local community organizations, CVS promoted telehealth options and mobile clinic visits to reach populations with difficulty accessing care.

Discussion Questions:

1- Regulatory Limitations and Patient Skepticism:

• How did CVS Health address patients' skepticism about using telemedicine or mobile clinics, which may have seemed less trustworthy than in-person visits?

• In what ways could CVS Health ensure that their marketing claims about telehealth and mobile clinics comply with healthcare marketing regulations while maintaining transparency and patient trust?

2- Disparities in Healthcare Access:

• How did CVS Health's campaign help address disparities in healthcare access, particularly in rural or underserved urban areas?

• What role can healthcare marketers play in bridging gaps in access to care, and how can they ensure that their messaging reaches the communities who need it the most?

3- Future Trends in Healthcare Marketing – Digital Transformation:

• How did CVS Health incorporate digital transformation into its marketing strategy to promote health and mobile clinics?

• What are some potential future trends in digital healthcare marketing that could further improve patient engagement, especially for underserved populations?

4- Hyper-Personalization in Healthcare Marketing:

• How could CVS Health use patient data (e.g., from wearables or health apps) to personalize marketing for their telehealth services and mobile clinics?

• What challenges do CVS face when implementing hyper-personalization, and how could they overcome them to improve patient engagement?

5- Emerging Technologies – AR/VR in Healthcare Marketing:

• CVS Health did not implement AR/VR, but how could these technologies enhance their telehealth services in the future? For example, how could VR be used to educate patients about how telehealth visits work or to simulate healthcare experiences?

• What role do emerging technologies like AR/VR play in shaping patient expectations and experiences, and how can healthcare marketers integrate these technologies into their campaigns to enhance patient education?

6- Predictive Analytics for Proactive Care:

•   How could CVS Health use predictive analytics to target at-risk patients and promote the preventive services available through their telehealth and mobile clinic offerings?

•   How would a campaign based on predictive analytics differ from traditional marketing efforts regarding patient engagement and long-term health outcomes?

Chapter 32: Self-Marketing in Healthcare and Non-Profit Sectors

32.1 Introduction to Self-Marketing: The Importance of Personal Branding

In today's competitive landscape, healthcare professionals face the challenge of standing out in a crowded field. While word-of-mouth referrals have long been the cornerstone of healthcare marketing, personal branding has become increasingly vital. Personal branding is developing and promoting your unique identity and expertise to differentiate yourself from others.

Take, for example, a cardiologist who consistently publishes educational YouTube videos about heart health. Not only does this help patients learn more about their condition, but it also establishes the cardiologist as a thought leader. This increased visibility can attract more patients, provide speaking opportunities, and even result in media appearances. A strong personal brand can provide ongoing marketing benefits that word-of-mouth alone cannot match.

32.2 Why You Should Market Yourself in the Healthcare Industry

In the healthcare industry, marketing yourself is not just about attracting more patients; it's about standing out in a crowded field, building trust, and creating lasting relationships. With the rise of digital platforms, patients increasingly search online for trustworthy healthcare providers. A strong personal brand helps you establish credibility and demonstrate your expertise, making it easier for potential patients to find you. Self-marketing also opens new opportunities, such as speaking engagements, collaborations with other healthcare professionals, and career advancements. By marketing yourself, you enhance your professional visibility and contribute to the broader healthcare community by educating and helping others. In a field driven by trust and reputation, marketing yourself allows you to position yourself as a reliable and compassionate expert in your specialty.

32.3 Developing a Self-Marketing Plan

Creating a self-marketing plan doesn't have to be complicated. Follow this simple outline to get started:

Step 1: Define What You Want to Share

Think about what makes you unique. This could be:

• Your area of expertise (e.g., pediatric care, diabetes management, mental health).

• Your values (e.g., patient care, compassion, wellness).

• Your personal story or journey in healthcare.

Step 2: Set Up Your Online Presence

• LinkedIn: Create a professional profile. Add your job experience, education, and certifications. Share short updates or articles related to your field.

• Instagram or Facebook: These platforms are great for sharing behind-the-scenes glimpses of your work. You can share tips on healthy living, managing stress, or common health myths.

Step 3: Start Sharing Helpful Content

• Health Tips: Post one simple health tip each week. For example, a nurse might post about the importance of hand washing or ways to reduce stress.

• Personal Insights: Share small stories from your daily work (without violating patient confidentiality). These could be about your challenges, experiences, or moments that made you proud.

Step 4: Ask for Patient Reviews

• Encourage satisfied patients to leave reviews online (Google, Healthgrades, etc.). A positive review from a patient who has had a valuable experience will help build trust with potential future patients.

Step 5: Network with Colleagues

• Online Communities: Join groups or forums related to your profession on LinkedIn or Facebook. You can learn from others, share advice, and build your professional network.

• Collaborate Locally: Work with colleagues in your area to promote health awareness, like hosting a small health talk or authoring articles for a local newsletter.

Step 6: Stay Consistent

• Post regularly, even if it's just once a week. Consistency is key to building a presence. You don't need to be on every social media platform, just the ones where your target audience (patients or peers) is most active.

32.4 Ethical Considerations in Self-Marketing

While marketing yourself is important, staying within ethical boundaries is essential. Healthcare professionals are trusted with people's health, so transparency and professionalism must always come first.

1. Avoid Over-Promotion

• Focus on educating and helping, not just selling your services. Marketing should be about building relationships and trust, not just attracting clients.

2. Respect Patient Privacy

• Never share personal patient details without consent. To share a patient success story, ensure anonymity or get written permission.

3. Transparency

• Be honest about your credentials and expertise. False advertising can damage your reputation and trust.

32.5 Quick Check

1. What is personal branding in the healthcare industry?

a) Creating a marketing plan for a healthcare facility
b) Developing and promoting your unique identity and expertise to differentiate yourself from others
c) Advertising healthcare services through third-party providers
d) Focusing only on traditional word-of-mouth referrals

2. Why is self-marketing important for healthcare professionals?

a) To attract more patients and create lasting relationships
b) To focus solely on profit-making
c) To avoid digital platforms
d) To rely solely on word-of-mouth referrals

3. What is the first step in developing a self-marketing plan?

a) Set up your online presence
b) Start sharing helpful content
c) Define what you want to share
d) Ask for patient reviews

4. Which platforms are suggested for healthcare professionals to establish a professional online presence?

a) Snapchat
b) Instagram or Facebook
c) LinkedIn
d) TikTok

5. What content is suggested for healthcare professionals to share on social media?

a) Promotional material only
b) Behind-the-scenes glimpses of their work and health tips
c) Patient medical records
d) Advertisements for expensive treatments

6. Why is it important to ask patients for reviews in healthcare marketing?

a) To focus solely on attracting new patients
b) Positive reviews help build trust with potential future patients
c) To increase the number of appointments booked
d) To promote only paid services

7. What is an ethical consideration in self-marketing for healthcare professionals?

a) Over-promoting services to increase patient numbers
b) Sharing personal patient details without consent
c) Being transparent about credentials and expertise
d) Posting exaggerated claims about treatment success rates

8. What is the recommended approach to marketing in healthcare?

a) Focusing only on selling services and products
b) Prioritizing patient education, relationship building, and trust
c) Ignoring social media platforms
d) Using misleading advertisements for treatments

Correct answers

1- b

2- a

3- c

4- c

5- b

6- b

7- c

8- b

32.6 Case: 2 Docs Talk – Building Trust Through Podcasting

2 Docs Talk is a podcast created by Dr. Kendall Britt and Dr. Amy Rogers, two Texas-based doctors, focusing on relevant healthcare topics for professionals and the public. The episodes, lasting 15 minutes, cover subjects such as hospital policies and personal healthcare tips, with the primary goal of helping listeners make more informed health decisions.

Their podcast served its primary educational purpose and increased the popularity of doctors and their practices. By addressing healthcare issues casually and approachable, they made complex topics more accessible, which helped build trust with their audience. As a result, their practices experienced a surge in new patients.

Given that healthcare in the U.S. is a significant concern for the working population, and self-care can be overwhelming with busy schedules, the podcast served as a valuable alternative for promoting healthy conversations and making healthcare more approachable. The innovative use of podcasts in healthcare marketing became one of the industry's most notable examples.

1. Importance of Personal Branding:

• How did the podcast, 2 Docs Talk, contribute to Dr. Britt and Dr. Rogers' branding, and what strategies did they use to stand out from other healthcare professionals?

• What role did the podcast play in building credibility and establishing trust with their audience?

2. Building Trust and Standing Out:

• In a competitive healthcare landscape, how did the 2 Docs Talk podcast help Dr. Britt and Dr. Rogers differentiate themselves from other healthcare providers?

• What ways can healthcare professionals use similar self-marketing tactics (like podcasts or social media) to build trust and increase their visibility?

3. Ethical Considerations in Self-Marketing:

• What ethical considerations should Dr. Britt and Dr. Rogers have considered while using their podcast as a marketing tool, particularly regarding patient privacy and transparency?

• How can healthcare professionals ensure that their branding efforts align with ethical guidelines, such as avoiding over-promotion or maintaining patient confidentiality?

4. Effective Use of Digital Platforms:

• How did the podcast format serve as a valuable digital platform for reaching their audience, and what other digital platforms could they have used to expand their outreach further?

• How can healthcare professionals leverage digital media (like podcasts, YouTube, or blogs) to educate the public and build a loyal patient base?

5. Content Strategy and Consistency:

• What content strategy did Dr. Britt and Dr. Rogers use to engage their audience through their podcast, and how can other healthcare professionals apply similar strategies to create consistent, helpful content?

• How important is consistency in content creation for healthcare professionals aiming to build their brand? What potential challenges might they face in staying consistent with their marketing efforts?

6. Opportunities for Growth and Networking:

• How did the podcast offer Dr. Britt and Dr. Rogers opportunities for professional networking, collaborations, or public speaking engagements?

• What are the benefits of networking through platforms like podcasts, and how can it lead to new professional opportunities and further enhance a healthcare professional's brand.?

Bibliography:

• American Marketing Association (2017). Definition of Marketing. Retrieved from ama.org

• Kotler, P., & Keller, K. L. (2016). Marketing Management (15th ed.). Pearson.

• Lamb, C. W., Hair, J. F., & McDaniel, C. (2021). MKTG. Cengage Learning.

• Thomas, R. K. (2008). Health Services Marketing: A Practitioner's Guide. Springer.

• Sharma, S., Gupta, A., & Singh, R. (2020). Personal Selling in Health and Medicine: Using Sales Agents to Engage Audiences. ResearchGate.

• Corbin, C. L., Kelley, S. W., & Schwartz, R. W. (2001). Concepts in service marketing for healthcare professionals. The American Journal of Surgery, 181(1), 1-7. https://doi.org/10.1016/S0002-9610(00)00535-3

• Akob, M., Yantahin, M., Ilyas, G. B., Hala, Y., & Putra, A. H. P. K. (2021). Element of marketing: SERVQUAL toward patient loyalty in the private hospital sector. Journal of Asian Finance, Economics and Business, 8(1), 419-430. https://doi.org/10.13106/jafeb.2021.vol8.no1.419

• Khalaf, A. M. K., Al-Qarni, A. A. A., Alsharqi, O., & Qalai, D. A. (2013). The impact of marketing mix strategy on hospital performance measured by patient satisfaction: An empirical investigation on the perspective of Jeddah private sector hospital senior managers. International Journal of Marketing Studies, 5(6), 210-220. https://doi.org/10.5539/ijms.v5n6p210

• Çağlıyor, S., Tosun, P., & Uray, N. (2022). Communicating Value in Healthcare Marketing from a Social Media Perspective. In New Perspectives in Operations Research and Management Science (pp. 143–170). Springer Nature.

- Hugar, G. G. (2021). Patient-centric marketing in healthcare: Enhancing consumer experience in a digital age. International Journal of Food and Nutritional Sciences, 10(3), 811-813. https://ijfans.org/uploads/paper/3a7dfd8b91e70233b0b953a524b3ca9a.pdf

- Fillis, I., & Michael, J. (2021). Charity Marketing: Contemporary Issues, Research, and Practice. Retrieved from ResearchGate: https://www.researchgate.net/publication/356070903_Charity_Marketing_Contemporary_Issues_Research_and_Practice

- Nnamdi, M. (2024). Predictive analytics in healthcare. American University Washington D.C. Retrieved from https://www.researchgate.net/publication/379478196_Predictive_Analytics_in_Healthcare

- On life Health. (2019). N of 1: The power of hyper-personalization. Retrieved from https://www.onlifehealth.com/wp-content/uploads/2019/10/Onlife-Health-N-of-1-The-Power-of-Hyper-Personalization.pdf

- Nguyen, T. T. H., Tran, T. T., & Nguyen, T. H. (2016). Fuzzy indicators for customer retention. International Journal of Engineering Business Management. Retrieved from https://www.researchgate.net/publication/309958920_Fuzzy_indicators_for_customer_retention

- Ng, H. S., & Kee, D. M. H. (2011). Key intangible performance indicators (KIPs) for organizational success: The literature review. International Journal of Asian Business and Information Management, 2(3), 1-14. https://doi.org/10.4018/IJABIM.2011070101

Section Four:

Emotional Intelligence in Healthcare

Chapter 33: Introduction to Emotional Intelligence (EI)

33.1 Definition and Key Components of EI

Emotional intelligence (EI) is recognizing, understanding, managing, and influencing emotions in oneself and others (Goleman, 1995). The concept of EI suggests that emotions play a crucial role in decision-making, interpersonal interactions, and overall psychological well-being. It emphasizes cognitive intelligence, emotional awareness, and regulation, which are key to personal and professional success.

Daniel Goleman (1995), a pioneer in the field of EI, proposed five core components that define emotional intelligence:

1. **Self-awareness** – the ability to recognize and understand one's emotions and their effect on thoughts and behavior. High self-awareness allows individuals to manage their emotional responses in various situations, making it easier to navigate both personal and professional challenges (Goleman, 1995). It contributes significantly to leadership effectiveness, as leaders must be aware of their emotional state to make informed decisions (Karimi et al., 2021).

2. **Self-regulation** – the ability to manage and control emotional impulses, particularly in complex or high-pressure situations. This competency is vital for maintaining emotional stability in healthcare environments with everyday stress and high-stakes situations. Leaders with strong self-regulation are better at controlling their reactions, avoiding hasty decisions, and maintaining professionalism (Freshman & Rubino, 2002).

3. **Motivation**—This component involves being driven to achieve goals for intrinsic reasons and maintaining a positive outlook despite challenges. Motivated individuals often inspire and influence others, fostering a productive and resilient environment (Goleman, 1995). In healthcare leadership, motivated leaders can inspire their teams, enhancing performance and patient care (Chaudry et al., 2021).

4. Empathy – the ability to understand and share the feelings of others. Empathy is crucial for healthcare leaders and practitioners, enabling them to build trust with patients and staff. Understanding others' emotions improves patient care and team dynamics (Goleman et al., 2002). Empathetic healthcare leaders are more attuned to the needs of their team and patients, which is critical in high-stress, high-emotion environments like healthcare (Mann, 2005).

5. Social skills – managing relationships and positively influencing others. Leaders with strong social skills are adept at communication, conflict resolution, and team building, essential in healthcare settings where collaboration is key. Practical social skills enable healthcare leaders to foster an environment of cooperation, engagement, and shared responsibility (Karimi et al., 2021). Leaders who excel in social skills can lead teams more effectively, improving team cohesion and patient care outcomes (Chaudry et al., 2021).

These five components work synergistically to enhance both personal and professional effectiveness. Emotional intelligence enables individuals to navigate complex interpersonal relationships and difficult emotional situations more quickly and confidently. Applying EI can improve patient care, reduce stress, and more effective leadership (Salovey & Mayer, 1990).

Role of EI in Personal and Professional Life

In personal life, EI fosters better emotional regulation, helping individuals maintain healthier relationships and cope with stress and challenges. Individuals with high emotional intelligence are generally more self-aware and more able to manage their emotions effectively, leading to better outcomes in their relationships (Goleman, 1995). They can navigate conflicts more successfully, making them better partners, friends, and family members.

Emotional intelligence (EI) is critical in building effective teams, leading with empathy, and making sound decisions. For healthcare leaders, high EI fosters a supportive environment where staff are more likely to feel valued, engaged, and motivated (Freshman & Rubino, 2002). Healthcare leaders with strong emotional intelligence are more capable of making decisions prioritizing the well-being of patients and staff, improving overall organizational performance (Karimi et al., 2021).

Healthcare environments are particularly demanding, and leaders with high EI can positively influence employee engagement and reduce burnout. Studies show leaders with strong emotional intelligence tend to have more engaged teams and better patient outcomes (Karimi et al., 2021). Empathy, one of the core components of EI, allows healthcare leaders to understand the emotional needs of patients and staff, fostering trust and support (Goleman et al., 2002). EI contributes significantly to effective leadership, driving team collaboration, reducing stress, and improving performance, making it a key skill for healthcare professionals (Mann, 2005).

Moreover, EI aids in managing conflict, a frequent challenge in healthcare settings. Leaders with high EI are skilled at diffusing tension and resolving conflicts constructively, which helps maintain a harmonious work environment and improves overall team performance (Karimi et al., 2021). This is especially important in healthcare organizations, where stress, burnout, and interpersonal conflict can directly impact patient care and employee retention.

In summary, emotional intelligence is vital for healthcare leaders, helping them navigate their personal lives and professional roles effectively. By enhancing relationships, decision-making, and overall team performance, EI supports better patient care and contributes to a more positive organizational culture.

33.2 The Role of Emotions in Healthcare

Emotions in Healthcare Settings

Healthcare environments are inherently emotionally intense, involving life-and-death situations, trauma, and ongoing care. Understanding the role of emotions in healthcare settings is crucial for both healthcare providers and leaders. Emotions influence decision-making, interactions with patients, and collaboration among staff. Emotional intelligence (EI) allows healthcare professionals to manage these emotions effectively, ensuring they remain composed in high-pressure situations and provide the best possible care for their patients.

Emotional regulation, a component of EI, is particularly essential in healthcare, as it enables staff to respond appropriately to stressful and emotionally charged situations. According to Dewettinck & Buyens (2014), healthcare professionals with high EI are more adept at managing the emotional challenges inherent in their work, including dealing with patient grief, distress, and anxiety. These professionals can maintain composure and focus, critical for ensuring patient safety and effective care.

Leaders with high EI can create a supportive and empathetic work environment that positively impacts staff well-being. A supportive work culture reduces burnout, fosters team collaboration, and enhances communication, all contributing to better patient care (Higgs & Rowland, 2018). By setting an example of emotional awareness and regulation, leaders can promote a positive emotional climate that encourages empathy, resilience, and job satisfaction among healthcare professionals.

33.3 Case Studies Illustrating Emotional Challenges

33.3.1 Case Study 1: Emotional Burnout in Nurses During the COVID-19 Pandemic

Overview

During the COVID-19 pandemic, healthcare workers faced unprecedented emotional challenges, with nurses particularly vulnerable to emotional burnout. High patient mortality rates, long working hours, and constant fear of contracting the virus created an emotionally taxing environment for many frontline healthcare workers.

Emotional Challenges

Nurses experienced significant emotional burnout, including feelings of helplessness, anxiety, and emotional exhaustion. Many reported difficulties managing their emotions while providing care to critically ill patients, especially when faced with frequent patient deaths. The emotional strain was compounded by isolation from family and friends due to quarantine measures.

Impact on Healthcare

Emotional exhaustion and burnout led to a decline in care quality, reduced empathy toward patients, and difficulties in decision-making. Nurses began to show signs of disengagement and had a more challenging time connecting with patients, impacting patient satisfaction and treatment adherence. Some even considered leaving the profession, citing emotional strain as a key factor.

Response and Resolution

Hospitals responded by implementing mental health support programs, offering counseling, and training staff in emotional intelligence to help manage stress and burnout. Teams were also encouraged to debrief and share their emotional experiences. Several hospitals provided EI-focused workshops to help nurses understand and manage their emotions effectively, leading to better team dynamics and patient care.

33.3.2 Case Study 2: Empathy Fatigue in Pediatric Care

Overview

In pediatric care settings, healthcare professionals often form deep emotional connections with their young patients and their families. However, emotional fatigue can develop, mainly when dealing with chronically ill or terminally ill children.

Emotional Challenges

A pediatric nurse in a children's hospital frequently cared for young patients undergoing long-term treatment for life-threatening illnesses. She reported experiencing empathy fatigue, characterized by emotional numbness and a diminished ability to empathize with her patients' suffering. This emotional detachment occurred as a protective mechanism, as she could no longer emotionally invest in every patient's struggle without feeling overwhelmed.

Impact on Healthcare

Emotional exhaustion caused by empathy fatigue led to decreased patient satisfaction. The nurse's ability to engage emotionally with patients and their families diminished, impacting the quality of communication and emotional support provided. Patients' families noted a lack of emotional connection during care.

Response and Resolution

Recognizing the emotional strain on staff, the hospital implemented structured emotional support programs for caregivers, including sessions on managing emotional labor, building resilience, and improving empathy through EI training. Nurses were encouraged to focus on self-care and participate in peer support groups to share experiences and alleviate stress. The intervention helped improve emotional engagement and patient-family relationships.

33.3.3 Case Study 3: Emotional Labor in Emergency Room (ER) Staff

Overview

Emergency room (ER) staff face high-pressure situations with limited emotional processing time. They are often required to display a level of emotional control, even in the face of traumatic events. Emotional labor, where staff must manage their emotions to meet the expectations of their role, can lead to significant emotional strain.

Emotional Challenges

An ER doctor reported feeling emotional distress from the high volume of trauma cases he encountered daily. Despite his professional training, he felt emotionally drained from dealing with critical cases of gunshot wounds, traffic accidents, and trauma victims. Emotional labor required him to suppress his emotions, especially in situations where patients' chances of survival were minimal. Over time, this emotional suppression led to stress, anxiety, and a sense of emotional detachment from patients.

Impact on Healthcare

The emotional toll led to decreased job satisfaction, lower morale, and difficulty maintaining high levels of patient care. The doctor's emotional disconnect affected his communication with patients and their families as he struggled to provide compassionate care in stressful circumstances. This also impacted the team's morale, with staff experiencing emotional fatigue and a lack of emotional support.

Response and Resolution

To address these emotional challenges, the hospital introduced regular debriefing sessions after high-stress events. Additionally, ER staff participated in emotional intelligence workshops to help them develop coping strategies for managing emotional labor. The hospital also instituted mindfulness programs and relaxation techniques to assist staff in managing stress. As a result, ER staff felt better equipped to handle emotional challenges, improving staff well-being and patient care.

33.3.4 Case Study 4: Emotional Intelligence Training for Healthcare Leaders

Overview

A large healthcare organization recognized the importance of emotional intelligence (EI) in leadership, particularly in managing stress and navigating the emotional challenges of running a hospital.

Emotional Challenges

The hospital's leadership team often struggled with managing staff morale, especially during crises such as mass casualty events or outbreaks of infectious diseases. As they were stressed, leaders found maintaining a positive work environment challenging. This created an atmosphere of emotional tension that affected team cohesion and decision-making.

Impact on Healthcare

The lack of emotional regulation at the leadership level led to poor communication and reduced team collaboration. Healthcare workers were less likely to seek support from their managers, and patient care suffered due to the emotional disconnect within the team.

Response and Resolution

The hospital implemented EI training for leaders, focusing on developing self-awareness, self-regulation, empathy, and social skills. The training helped leaders understand their own emotions and those of their teams, leading to better stress and emotional challenge management. Leaders were able to model emotional intelligence in their interactions with staff, improving morale and communication across the organization. As a result, staff engagement and patient satisfaction improved.

Chapter 34: EI and Quality of Care

34.1 Impact of EI on Healthcare Quality and Patient Care

Emotional intelligence (EI) profoundly influences healthcare quality and patient care. Leaders and healthcare providers with high levels of EI tend to foster positive relationships with patients and colleagues, enhancing patient outcomes and overall care quality. Recognizing, understanding, and managing emotions in oneself and others is essential for promoting a supportive and empathetic environment in healthcare settings.

Studies have shown that emotionally intelligent leaders create environments prioritizing empathy, compassion, and clear communication, all of which are linked to improved patient outcomes (Shapiro & Tarrant, 2015). EI also enhances the ability of healthcare workers to remain composed and responsive in high-pressure situations, which can improve care delivery, reduce medical errors, and ultimately result in better patient experiences (Goleman, 1995).

Karimi et al. (2021) highlight that EI significantly predicts employee well-being and patient care quality. Healthcare professionals with higher EI can better manage stress and emotional challenges, leading to a positive work environment that encourages collaboration and patient-centered care. This, in turn, improves patient outcomes, as emotionally intelligent workers are more empathetic, engaged, and responsive to patient needs.

Building rapport with patients through emotional awareness and regulation enhances the quality of care provided in healthcare settings. Empathetic care has been linked to improved patient satisfaction, better adherence to treatment plans, and a greater likelihood of patients feeling understood and valued (Shapiro & Tarrant, 2015).

34.2 Role of Empathy and Communication in Healthcare Quality

Empathy and effective communication are central components of EI that directly affect healthcare quality. Empathy enables healthcare professionals to understand and share the emotional experiences of their patients, which is critical for building trust and fostering a therapeutic relationship. Healthcare workers who exhibit empathy are more likely to provide patient-centered care, where the patient's needs, preferences, and values are central to care delivery (Mayer & Salovey, 2004).

Another key element of EI is effective communication, crucial in ensuring patients fully understand their conditions, treatment options, and the course of care. Healthcare professionals who can communicate clearly and empathetically help patients feel more comfortable discussing their concerns, which improves patient compliance and reduces misunderstandings (Mayer & Salovey, 2004).

Karimi et al. (2021) emphasize that integrating EI into healthcare practice improves emotional resilience among staff and fosters open communication, directly benefiting patient care. The authors note that emotionally intelligent healthcare workers are more likely to engage in compassionate communication with patients, enhancing the patient-provider relationship and improving treatment outcomes.

Moreover, emotionally intelligent leaders in healthcare organizations promote a culture of empathy and communication by modeling these behaviors, supporting staff development, and ensuring that patient interactions are characterized by respect and understanding. As a result, staff and patients benefit from a healthcare environment where emotional intelligence is prioritized, improving care quality and patient satisfaction (Karimi et al., 2021).

34.3 Emotional Intelligence (EI) and Employee Well-being

Emotional Intelligence (EI) is pivotal in enhancing employee well-being, especially in high-stress environments like healthcare. EI helps healthcare leaders create a supportive work environment, reduce stress, improve job satisfaction, and foster collaboration. This module delves into how EI can positively influence employee well-being, reduce burnout, enhance job engagement, and improve team dynamics, all of which contribute to improved healthcare outcomes.

The Link Between EI and Employee Well-being

Emotional intelligence refers to recognizing, understanding, and regulating emotions in oneself and others. In healthcare settings, EI is a crucial skill for leaders, as it helps them manage the emotional demands of the workplace, support employee well-being, and ensure positive organizational outcomes.

• Defining Employee Well-being: Employee well-being in healthcare is a multifaceted concept that includes emotional, physical, and psychological health. Well-being is associated with job satisfaction, stress levels, engagement, and overall mental health (Carmeli, 2003).

• EI and Well-being: Employees with high EI are more likely to have better interpersonal relationships, which is essential in collaborative healthcare settings. High EI enables employees to manage stress, build resilience, and cope with the emotional challenges inherent in healthcare work. EI also supports emotional regulation, leading to lower levels of burnout and increased well-being (Bar-On, 2006).

Impact on Burnout and Stress Reduction

Healthcare workers, often at high risk of burnout due to the demanding nature of their jobs, can benefit significantly from EI. It provides much-needed relief, helping leaders identify early burnout signs, manage team stress, and foster a work culture that reduces emotional exhaustion.

• Identifying Signs of Burnout: Emotional intelligence is a practical tool for healthcare leaders and managers to recognize the early signs of burnout, such as disengagement, emotional exhaustion, and increased absenteeism. Prompt identification of these indicators is crucial, as burnout often leads to a diminished sense of accomplishment and reduced empathy toward patients (Carmeli, 2003).

• Managing Stress Within Teams: Leaders with high EI are crucial in creating a supportive and emotionally safe work environment. They understand the impact of stress and can implement strategies to alleviate it, such as providing emotional support, ensuring adequate work-life balance, and encouraging open communication (Bar-On, 2006). High EI leaders also promote stress management practices, such as mindfulness or relaxation exercises, to help healthcare workers cope with high-pressure situations. This practical application of EI in managing team stress is a key factor in improving team dynamics and organizational performance.

• Reducing Stress and Promoting Resilience: EI plays a significant role in helping healthcare professionals regulate emotions, improving resilience, and lowering stress levels. Employees with high EI are better equipped to manage their emotions during stressful situations, contributing to overall well-being and job satisfaction. Studies have shown that employees with high EI report feeling more in control of their work and experience lower levels of burnout (Bar-On, 2006). This underscores the importance of EI in promoting resilience and reducing stress, enhancing job satisfaction and team performance.

34.4 Emotional Intelligence (EI)'s Influence on Organizational Performance

Emotional Intelligence (EI) profoundly affects healthcare organizations' performance, influencing employee well-being and key financial and operational metrics. This module explores how EI impacts organizational success, particularly financial performance, healthcare quality, and operational efficiency. By leveraging academic studies and evidence, we will discuss the relationship between EI and organizational performance, especially in healthcare environments, demonstrating the importance of EI competencies in leadership roles.

The Financial and Performance Benefits of EI

EI's influence on healthcare organizations extends beyond individual well-being to impact organizational performance across several dimensions, including financial outcomes, patient satisfaction, and operational effectiveness.

How EI Drives Organizational Efficiency and Growth

In the healthcare sector, leadership is a key driver of organizational performance. Leaders with high EI can make better decisions, manage resources more effectively, and foster a culture of collaboration, which contributes to an organization's growth and success. EI competencies, such as self-awareness, empathy, and emotional regulation, enhance decision-making and help leaders create an environment that improves organizational efficiency.

• Enhanced Decision-Making: EI empowers healthcare leaders to integrate emotional and cognitive intelligence, leading to more informed and effective decision-making processes. According to Vasilenko and Bogdanova (2020), emotionally intelligent leaders can better navigate complex healthcare environments, resulting in decisions that balance patient care with organizational goals. This empowerment fosters financial growth and stability.

• Resource Management and Growth: Leaders with high EI are skilled at managing organizational resources effectively. EI helps healthcare leaders allocate resources more efficiently by understanding team dynamics and managing stress. Boyatzis (2008) highlights that EI competencies—such as emotional self-regulation and empathy—are directly linked to financial success in leadership roles. In healthcare organizations, where resource allocation can significantly impact economic performance, these competencies are crucial in sustaining organizational growth.

• Strategic Leadership and Organizational Resilience: EI supports strategic leadership by fostering emotional attunement to the needs of both employees and patients. Leaders with EI are more likely to foster positive relationships, build trust, and ensure that the organization's strategic objectives align with patient care goals. As Boyatzis (2008) suggests, EI competencies are fundamental in achieving long-term growth and stability, allowing leaders to adjust to changing environments and organizational challenges.

Role in Improving Healthcare Performance Metrics

Performance metrics, such as patient satisfaction, clinical outcomes, and operational efficiency, are crucial for assessing the success of healthcare organizations. EI significantly impacts these metrics, improving patient care and organizational effectiveness.

• Improved Patient Satisfaction: EI-driven leadership directly influences patient satisfaction, as leaders foster a culture where employees are motivated, emotionally aware, and empathetic. Chaudry et al. (2020) emphasize that emotionally intelligent leaders improve patient satisfaction by encouraging healthcare professionals to engage empathetically with patients. This results in more effective communication, a key factor in patient satisfaction. By understanding and applying EI, leaders can feel accomplished and successful.

• Enhanced Clinical Outcomes: Leaders with high EI promote collaboration, communication, and teamwork—essential elements for improving clinical outcomes. Mayer et al. (2002) found that emotionally intelligent leaders help foster a culture of collaboration, improving decision-making and patient care. By managing emotions effectively, these leaders can motivate their teams, leading to better clinical results.

• Financial Control and Risk Management: Emotional intelligence also influences financial performance in healthcare. According to Childs (2019), EI helps mitigate financial risk in healthcare practices by ensuring that leaders and administrative staff can manage the emotional complexities of financial oversight. By using EI competencies to make informed financial decisions, healthcare organizations can avoid financial mismanagement and sustain fiscal health.

Tipping Points of EI Competencies and Financial Performance

Boyatzis's (2008) research reveals the significant link between EI competencies and financial performance in leadership roles. Boyatzis's study of leaders in a multinational consulting firm shows that the frequency with which leaders demonstrate EI competencies strongly predicts their economic success. This study introduces the concept of "tipping points" of EI—indicating that a certain threshold of EI competencies must be reached for leaders to demonstrate outstanding financial performance.

• Tipping Points of EI: Boyatzis (2008) uses tipping point analysis to explore how much of a specific EI competency is necessary for exceptional financial performance. His research found that leaders who demonstrate EI competencies consistently outperform their peers financially. This finding underscores the importance of EI in leadership roles, especially in dynamic and high-stakes environments like healthcare.

• Emotional Intelligence as a Predictor of Success: Boyatzis (2008) shows that emotional intelligence is a dominant predictor of financial performance, with EI competencies accounting for most (13 out of 14) of the competencies that predict leadership success. These findings suggest that EI is crucial in managing teams, improving operational efficiency, and driving financial outcomes.

Chapter 35: Emotional Intelligence (EI) Competencies for Healthcare Leaders

Emotional Intelligence (EI) is fundamental to effective leadership, particularly in healthcare environments, where the demands are high, and the emotional stakes are even higher. In this module, we will explore the core EI competencies that healthcare leaders must develop, the strategies to enhance these competencies, and practical tools that can be employed to build EI skills. We will demonstrate from relevant academic sources how EI competencies improve leadership effectiveness, promote a positive work culture, foster better patient outcomes, and support team cohesion.

35.1 Core EI Competencies for Healthcare Leaders

Healthcare leadership involves managing diverse teams, making critical decisions, and providing empathetic care in high-pressure situations. The core EI competencies are essential for healthcare leaders to ensure they are well-equipped to handle these challenges. These competencies include self-awareness, self-regulation, motivation, empathy, and social skills.

Self-awareness and Self-regulation

• Self-awareness is recognizing one's emotions and impact on others. For healthcare leaders, self-awareness enables them to stay grounded under pressure, preventing emotional reactions from hindering decision-making. A self-aware healthcare leader can understand their emotional triggers, maintain composure in challenging situations, and model emotional stability for their teams (Goleman, 1995). This competency is critical in healthcare settings where stress is a shared experience.

• Self-regulation refers to managing and controlling emotions, especially in difficult situations. Self-regulation enables leaders to handle high-pressure environments, remain calm in crises, and avoid impulsive decisions that could harm the organization or patient care. Goleman (1995) asserts that self-regulation is vital in managing emotional responses, such as frustration or stress, which are prevalent in fast-paced healthcare settings.

Healthcare leaders who master these competencies can easily navigate complex interpersonal and organizational dynamics, ensuring that their leadership style fosters a culture of respect, professionalism, and emotional balance.

• Motivation is a driving force behind a leader's ability to maintain focus, set and achieve goals, and inspire others to perform at their best. Highly motivated leaders set clear expectations and model positive behaviors, encouraging their teams to pursue excellence in patient care and organizational success (Boyatzis, 1982). Motivation is fundamental in healthcare settings, where leaders must constantly inspire their teams to achieve high standards of care despite challenges.

Motivated healthcare leaders also exhibit a strong commitment to continuous improvement and are driven by a desire to achieve personal and organizational goals. This competency creates a motivating work environment that encourages healthcare professionals to engage in their work with passion and dedication.

• Empathy involves understanding and sharing the feelings of others. For healthcare leaders, empathy is vital in building rapport with patients, staff, and other stakeholders. Empathy fosters trust and encourages open communication, which is essential for effective leadership and teamwork (Boyatzis, 1982). Leaders who exhibit empathy can listen attentively to their teams' concerns, support staff in their emotional needs, and create a caring and compassionate work environment.

• Social skills involve managing relationships, communicating effectively, and influencing others. In healthcare, social skills help leaders create a cohesive, collaborative environment where team members feel valued and motivated. These skills are essential for conflict resolution, building trust, and maintaining positive relationships with patients, staff, and peers. Leaders with strong social skills can facilitate cooperation, which is particularly important in multidisciplinary healthcare teams (Goleman, 1995).

35.2 Developing EI Competency

While some individuals may naturally possess high EI, healthcare leaders can enhance their EI competencies through dedicated strategies and continuous learning. Research has shown that EI can be developed through self-reflection, mindfulness, and consistent practice (Goleman et al., 2002).

Strategies to Improve EI Through Self-reflection and Continuous Learning

• Self-reflection: Self-reflection is a key practice in developing EI. Leaders who engage in regular self-reflection gain insight into their emotional triggers, thought patterns, and behaviors, which allows them to improve their emotional responses in future situations. This ongoing reflection helps leaders become more attuned to their emotions and impact on others, enhancing their ability to lead with empathy and emotional intelligence (Goleman et al., 2002).

• Mindfulness Practices: Mindfulness, which involves staying present and aware in the moment, is another powerful tool for enhancing EI. Studies have shown that mindfulness practices can improve self-awareness, emotional regulation, and empathy (Dott et al., 2025). Healthcare leaders who engage in mindfulness practices are better able to manage stress, maintain emotional stability, and respond thoughtfully to the needs of their teams and patients.

• Continuous Professional Development: Continuous learning is essential for the ongoing development of EI. Healthcare leaders must commit to professional development by attending training programs, workshops, and seminars on emotional intelligence (Dott et al., 2025). These learning opportunities provide leaders with the skills and strategies to manage emotions, enhance team collaboration, and improve patient outcomes.

35.3 Tools and Exercises to Build EI Skills

Healthcare leaders can utilize various tools and exercises to develop EI competencies further. These practical exercises help reinforce key EI skills, enabling leaders to apply emotional intelligence more effectively in real-world situations.

Journaling and Emotional Check-ins

- Journaling is a valuable tool for improving self-awareness and emotional regulation. By reflecting on daily experiences and emotions, leaders can identify patterns in their emotional responses and recognize areas for growth. Journaling also helps leaders track their progress over time, which is essential for maintaining emotional awareness (Goleman, 1995).

- Emotional Check-ins involve taking brief moments throughout the day to assess one's emotional state. By regularly checking in with their emotions, leaders can ensure they are aware of their feelings and can manage them effectively. This practice promotes emotional regulation, allowing leaders to respond to situations with excellent composure and clarity (Goleman et al., 2002).

35.4 Role-Playing and Feedback Exercises

- Role-playing exercises help healthcare leaders practice applying their EI competencies in simulated scenarios. Leaders can develop emotional responses and communication strategies by acting out difficult situations in a safe environment. Role-playing also allows leaders to gain valuable feedback from others, which can enhance their self-awareness and interpersonal skills (Russ et al., 2020).

- Feedback Exercises involve seeking constructive feedback from colleagues and team members regarding one's emotional responses and leadership style. Regular feedback helps leaders identify areas for improvement and refine their EI competencies (Cherry, 2020). Leaders who embrace feedback are better positioned to continuously develop their emotional intelligence and enhance their leadership effectiveness.

Conclusion: Being a Successful Healthcare Leader

Being a successful healthcare leader is not an easy task. The good news is that you can get better if you have worked hard towards that. No one is born as a successful leader. It takes a lot of interplaying factors that always start with the person. Whether in healthcare or any other field, a successful leader usually begins with a conscious decision from inside to be that person. Later, it is a long journey towards joint success because no one can be a successful leader without successful teams. Indeed, your most straightforward measure as a successful leader could be estimated through the impact you have achieved on successful teams.

It is worth mentioning that success itself as a concept is very relative among different persons. However, for the sake of this book, success is interpreted as having a successful impact on both the team and the organization. This could be displayed through a leader's actions and behaviors. Our actions and behaviors' cumulative impact determines whether we have succeeded or failed. Neither the organization nor the teams around us are affected by what we believe in, like, or dislike, but they are affected by our actions and behaviors.

To be a successful leader in healthcare, you should know your status and work on improved versions of three pillars: Your concepts about leadership and success, Your knowledge, and your skills. Together, these three pillars formulate your actions and behaviors as a leader.